The Boy From France

Praise for Hilary Freeman

'Camden comes to life on the page in this engaging and fun story of friendship and celebrities . . . with characters so realistic you feel you might bump into them at Camden Town tube!'

Chicklish

'The perfect choice for teenage girls (and their mums). Warm and witty, compelling and insightful.'

Sunday Express

'The characters are believable and the narrative is pacy . . . a good read.'

School Librarian

'A really good read . . . funny, yet realistic.'

Teen Titles

Camden Town Tales

The Boy From France

Hilary Freeman

Piccadilly Press • London

This book is dedicated to Mickaël Lorinquer,
my boy from France,
and to the memory of our beautiful daughter,
Elodie, who was born sleeping
on 26th September 2012
and who will always live in our hearts.

First published in Great Britain in 2013
by Piccadilly Press Ltd,
5 Castle Road, London NW1 8PR
www.piccadillypress.co.uk

A catalogue record for this book is available
from the British Library

ISBN: 978 1 84812 301 4 (paperback)
ISBN: 978 1 84812 302 1 (eBook)

1 3 5 7 9 10 8 6 4 2

Printed and bound by CPI Group (UK) Ltd, Croydon, CR0 4YY
Cover design by Simon Davis
Cover illustrations by Susan Hellard

Prologue

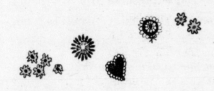

I turn into Paradise Avenue and glance at my watch. It's ten o'clock already. I've taken longer than I should have. Stupid me. Xavier will probably be up and about by now and Mum will be wondering where I've got to. She only wanted her prescription picking up but I got distracted in Boots, tried on some new nail varnish shades and wondered if she would notice if I bought one of them and gave her less change than was due. Anyone else would have made a quick decision but instead I ummed and ahhed for ages, swatching the shades, waiting for them to dry, changing my mind about which colour I liked best, and at least two or three times taking a bottle from the stand, then replacing it again. I guess

1

I wanted to treat myself for once, even though I knew I shouldn't. The sales assistant said the bright pink colour looked good on me, and I got as far as queuing up to pay for it, but then I felt guilty and didn't buy it after all. A waste of time. Stupid me.

It strikes me that something doesn't look right. Doesn't feel right. I must have walked up my street thousands of times since I was a little girl and, usually, I do it on autopilot, barely noticing the familiar buildings or the cars parked outside. And yet, today, I sense something new. The street isn't as quiet as it should be at this hour. There are too many people about, people standing outside their homes, waiting for something, watching something. I quicken my pace, trying to see past them, past the cars, wondering if the police have finally come to raid the art collective and throw the squatters out. But I can't see any police, or a police car, and as I pass the collective house it is as still and silent as I'd expect at this time on a Saturday, its windows blacked out as usual.

Now I can see that there's an ambulance parked up at the other end of the street. My end of the street. That isn't unusual. It's probably one of the old ladies from the almshouses, either being picked up or taken back from hospital. They're always falling over, or leaving their hobs on and setting off the fire alarm. But it doesn't explain why there are so many people on the street watching.

Mrs Richards, one of my neighbours, is standing on her doorstep as I pass.

'Hey, Mrs R, what's going on?' I ask, stopping for a moment. 'Is it the almshouses again?'

'I don't think so, Victoria,' she says, in a tone more excited than grave. 'An ambulance came tearing down here with its siren on and lights flashing about ten minutes ago. Someone's been hurt. That's all I know.'

'Thanks,' I say, nodding. 'How awful. I hope they're OK.'

As I turn to walk on, somebody grabs hold of my shoulder from behind. I jump, instinctively grasping my bag to my side, and swing around, ready to defend myself.

It's Xavier. My first feeling is one of relief – at least it isn't him who's hurt. Then I notice that his face is white. He mutters something in French and I can't tell if he's panicking or is angry with me.

'Slow down,' I say. 'I don't understand. Tell me in English.'

He grips my wrist, but not in a friendly way. His palm is moist and hot. 'Where 'ave you been? I called but you did not come.'

'I'm sorry, I was out. I had some chores to do. What's happened? Are you OK?'

He nods, but he doesn't seem OK. He looks scared.

A horrible realisation is beginning to dawn on me, but I don't want to acknowledge it.

'Come now,' he says. 'You must come now.' He pulls me along, past the onlookers, steering me around the cars that are parked across the kerb. My heart is pounding. I feel sick.

Now I know for certain: it's my house that's at the centre of the drama. My front door is wide open. The person in the ambulance must be my mum.

Chapter 1

Here Come The Boys

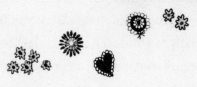

'As you all know, your French exchange students will be coming to stay next week,' says Miss Long who is, ironically, about four foot nine and the shape of a beach ball. 'And . . .' She pauses for maximum effect. '. . . as you'll no doubt be pleased to hear, the rumours are true: due to an administrative mix-up, this year, some of them will be boys.'

There's a murmur of excitement across the classroom. I go to an all girls' school, you see. We don't have the chance to meet boys very often.

'How many of them, Miss?' asks Lucy Reed, who is probably the loudest, most confident and – when it comes to boys – most experienced girl in our year. 'Who's going to get one?'

Rosie widens her eyes at me. 'She's only interested because she's been through every boy in London already,' she whispers, a little unkindly.

'Calm down, everyone. Shush!' says Miss Long. 'They're boys, not sweets. I won't be handing them out. There are five boys in total and they have already been allocated by the exchange programme organisers. You'll find a letter with the details of your exchange student in your pigeon-hole by the end of the day. Remember, this visit is not about romance, it's about improving your French.'

Half the class bursts into spontaneous giggles. I hear someone say, 'I think my French is pretty good already, Miss.'

Miss Long remains stony-faced. 'Improving your French language skills,' she clarifies. 'So you can put any other ideas out of your heads right now.'

But, of course, the prospect of snogging fit French boys is all anyone can think – or talk – about for the rest of the day. Everyone except me, that is. I honestly don't care if my French exchange student is a boy or a girl. I'm beginning to wish the exchange programme wasn't happening. I know that Mum can't really cope with putting someone up for a month right now, and she's only agreed because she thinks it will be good for my GCSE grade, and because she doesn't want me to feel left out.

My mum is sick, and it's not the type of illness you get better from. She's been ill for as long as I can remember but, lately, she's been getting worse. She's been in and out of hospital for treatments and now she can't walk properly any more. She keeps falling over. When we go out, she often has to use a stick or a walking frame, which she hates. She also has problems with her eyesight and her hands and she gets incredibly tired. Last year, she had to give up work, which meant Dad had to increase his hours, so he isn't around much. The upshot is, I have to do a lot more around the house than any of my friends. It's up to me to do the food shopping and a lot of the cleaning and cooking too. Sometimes, I even have to help Mum to get dressed or to have a shower. (I haven't told anyone that before, even Rosie and Sky, because it's embarrassing.) Don't get me wrong: I'm not complaining. I'm hardly a slave. It's not Mum's fault and I don't mind helping her, but it's hard to fit it all in with my coursework and seeing my friends. I already have to be super organised. How am I going to add in entertaining a French person too? And what if they don't understand?

The exchange trip letters appear in our pigeon-holes

sometime between lunch and the final period. I take mine out and open it cautiously, praying that whoever I'm getting is sweet and not too fussy and gets on with everybody. I've heard horror stories about exchange students who've stayed in their rooms, crying from homesickness for the entire month or, worse, who've taken an instant dislike to their host family and made their lives hell.

Rosie rushes over to me. 'Who've you got, then? I'm getting someone called Manon, who is – worse luck – one hundred per cent definitely a girl.'

I study my piece of paper. 'My exchange student is called Ex-avier Durand, and she's fifteen and from Nice.'

Rosie peers at my sheet. She grins. 'It's pronounced *neece*, not nice. And it's not ex-avier, it's *zav-ier*, like xylophone!' Her French has always been better than mine. 'Vix – Xavier a boy's name. You've got one of the boys!' She's so excited for me, you'd think I'd won the lottery. 'You jammy cow!'

I shrug. 'Oh, cool. I guess.'

Lucy has overheard and now she's dashing over. She snatches my exchange trip letter out of Rosie's hands. 'I can't believe it! Why did they give you one of the boys, Vix? You don't even like boys.'

'Yes she does,' says Rosie, sticking up for me. 'They probably didn't give you a boy because they wanted to make sure he went home in one piece. Without teeth marks.'

Lucy rolls her eyes. 'Whatever. God, what a waste. Sad for him that he's going to have such a boring time. Hey, do you wanna swap? Nobody has to know . . .'

Rosie grabs back the letter. 'I don't think so,' she says. 'Don't worry, Lucy, we'll make sure he has the *best* time. And we'll keep him out of your clutches.' She smiles at me.

I smile back, as enthusiastically as I can. I do like boys, just not the ones I know, who are, in my opinion, a waste of space – immature idiots with bum fluff, no style and absolutely nothing to say. Rosie's boyfriend Laurie is OK, but he's a bit older, and Max, who came to stay on our street last summer, was lovely but he had a thing for Rosie and only wanted to be friends with me. Typically. Most of the boys I've met are more like Sky's ex, Rich – they just muck you around and hurt you and then move on to the next girl. I can't imagine that French boys are any different. Except they have French accents. And they eat weird things like frogs' legs and snails and too much garlic, and *frites* instead of chips. At least French people are stylish. But, knowing my luck, I'll get the only French boy who really does wear a beret and a stripy top and ride a bicycle, like French people do in stupid cartoons. He'll probably bring a string of onions as a welcome gift.

I have been to France once, way back when I was a kid, but I can hardly remember anything about it, apart from seeing the Eiffel Tower and going shopping with Mum on the Champs-Elysées, when she could still walk without a stick. My French exchange student doesn't come from Paris, I remind myself, he comes from Nice. I have no idea what that's like. Actually, I have no idea where it is. France is a big country, much bigger than England. I guess I should look up Nice on the internet, so I can learn something about it before Xavier, or Ex-avier, or whatever he's called, arrives. I want to be able to make him feel at home, maybe buy some local food for him, and it would be good to have something to talk about. I hope his English is better than my French . . .

'What are you thinking about, Vix?' says Rosie. 'You're a million miles away.'

'Eh? Sorry. Nothing. Just wondering what Xavier will be like and stuff.'

She grins. 'Ah, so you are a teensy bit excited that you've got a sexy French boy coming to stay. I knew it!'

I blush. 'It's not like that – you know it isn't. Anyway, I bet you a million pounds he won't be sexy. And if he is, he'll like you, or Sky, not me. Like always. I just don't want him to have a rubbish time, what with my mum and everything. And I'm worried it'll be too much for her. She's only just come out of hospital.'

Rosie puts her arm around me. 'It'll be all right, Vix. You're worrying too much, thinking about all the what ifs before they've happened, like you always do. I've got a feeling he's going to be drop dead gorgeous. And why shouldn't he like you? You're drop dead gorgeous too.'

Chapter 2

My Secret Life

Drop dead gorgeous? Hardly. I don't have any complexes about the way I look, not like Sky, who has a thing about her nose (although she's a little better about it now), but I'm realistic – I'm not the type of girl who makes boys stop and stare. Boys like me, just not in *that* way.

I've never had a boyfriend. God, if I'm honest, I've never even kissed anyone. That information is top secret. Everybody thinks I have, and I've let them carry on thinking it – even Rosie and Sky, who believe they know all my secrets – because I'm almost fifteen and too embarrassed to admit that I haven't.

They think it happened at a party, last year, while we were all playing a stupid Spin-the-Bottle/truth-dare type game. Somehow – don't ask – I found myself having to get into a wardrobe with this guy, Robbie, from Sky's school, and we were supposed to stay in there for five minutes and snog. But we didn't. We were both too shy and we didn't really fancy each other, and I'm fairly certain he'd never kissed anybody before, either. So we stared at each other awkwardly for a while and then, I guess because he was wearing a T-shirt with a racing car on it, we ended up having a conversation about cars instead. He was impressed how much I knew about them because girls aren't supposed to be interested in that kind of thing, let alone be experts on the technical specifications of each Formula One circuit or car design. But I've always loved racing; I even played with cars instead of dolls when I was little. Rosie and Sky think my fascination with cars is weird and that it could partly explain why boys always want to be mates with me, and not my boyfriend. That, and the fact I think about things too much. Maybe they're right. Anyway, Robbie and I came out of the cupboard at that party, looking sheepish and smoothing down our clothes, like you're supposed to, and everybody thought we'd enjoyed five minutes of pashing, when we were really reviewing the previous week's *Top Gear*.

Fourteen, going on fifteen, and never been kissed –

what a cliché! I read advice pages online that say, 'It's fine never to have kissed anyone, however old you are . . . You'll do it when you're ready, when you meet the right guy . . . Be patient . . .' but none of it makes me feel any better. I feel like I'm the only girl in the world who hasn't done it, the only person who hasn't become a member of a club that I don't even know if I want to join. How can I know if I'll like it until I've done it? But if I do it just for the sake of doing it, with the wrong person, then I might not like it anyway. That would be pointless, wouldn't it? So I wait. And I wait. And I wait, for it to happen, somehow. And in the meantime, I pretend that I've already done it and that I'm not too fussed about doing it again. It means that some people, like Lucy Reed, think I don't like boys and others, like Sky and Rosie, think I'm just too choosy. Even my mum has started saying, 'When are you going to get a boyfriend, Victoria?' She refuses to call me Vix, however much I plead with her.

I was supposed to be going round to Rosie's tonight, but Dad's away on a business trip and Mum has had a bad day. Even though she hasn't asked, I think she wants some company, so I told Rosie I'd come tomorrow instead. Mum gets lonely, stuck at home on her own all day, while everybody else is out at work. She doesn't even like watching daytime TV, which would help. Since

I came home from school, I've done the vacuuming and popped to Sainsbury's to buy a few things, like toilet paper and pasta. Now we're having dinner and then I'll do some coursework. I should have time for an online chat with my friends before bed, if nothing else.

My cooking has got heaps better. I only used to be able to make beans on toast or omelette, so we ate a lot of microwave meals, but lately I've been watching *MasterChef* and finding recipes on the internet and I can rustle up a decent casserole or spaghetti bolognese or even a basic curry. Tonight we're having fish pie. It's a bit of an experiment and I'm not sure it's worked, but we're eating it anyway.

'So how was school today?' Mum asks, like she does every day. It's more of a ritual than a conversation.

'Fine.' I tell her, like I do every day. 'Same old, same old. You know . . .' And then I remember. 'Actually, I do have some news. About the exchange student.'

'Oh, yes?' Mum says. 'She's coming next week, isn't she?' She sighs. 'We'll have to get the spare room sorted.'

We both know that by 'we' she means 'me'.

'Yes. Except she's a he: Xavier. I hope that's OK. I've got a letter with all the details.'

'Sure,' she says. 'I didn't know it could be a boy.'

'Me neither. Miss Long sprang it on us this morning. Apparently there's been some administrative cock-up.

Too many boys and not enough takers at the boys' school, and not enough girls for us.'

'Well, it'll be nice to have a boy around the place for a change. Someone for your dad to talk about football to, and practise his French with. Where's he from?'

'From Nice. Wherever that is.'

'Ah.' She smiles. 'We went to Nice once on holiday, when you were a toddler. I don't suppose you remember.'

'No! I didn't realise I'd been there. I only remember Paris.'

Mum looks wistful. We haven't been on holiday for a couple of years, not since she starting getting worse. 'It's right in the South, near Italy. A bit like Brighton, in a way, with a long promenade and a stony beach. But there are palm trees and the sea is a beautiful blue, and it's lovely and hot and sunny there. I'm sure I must have some photos somewhere.' She moves as if to get out of her chair, but then remembers she can't do that as easily as she used to and grips on to the table to right herself again. Her stick is propped up against the wall, just out of reach. We both glance at it, but say nothing.

'I'll get them out for you later if you want. I'd like to see where he comes from,' I say eventually.

'I'd like that,' she replies. 'But you must do what you need to do first.'

I know she worries that I'm doing too much for her

now. She keeps asking about my grades, to make sure they're not slipping. I overheard her talking to Dad about how it was all becoming too difficult for me and he said perhaps they needed to think about getting a proper carer in. She said she wasn't ready for that. More worrying, they also discussed moving house. I keep telling her I'm coping fine. I really, really, really don't want to move. I like living on Paradise Avenue, so close to the centre of Camden Town. And I don't know what I'd do if Rosie and Sky weren't up the road.

After I've washed up, I help Mum on to the sofa and fetch a book for her. Then I go to my bedroom and do my maths coursework and then some English, but my mind isn't on it. Instead, I surf the web, looking at pictures of Nice. It seems so exotic, with its beaches and outdoor cafés, so different from grey-skied, noisy, hectic Camden. I wonder what Xavier will think of my area and my life and my friends. I wonder if he's ever been to London before. I wonder if he'll mind having to stay with a girl.

I turn on my instant messaging. Sky is online, waiting for me. She's super excited about my news, which, of course, Rosie has already told her.

So, she says, *you're getting a French boy. When's he arriving?*

Me: *Saturday afternoon. Dad's coming with me to pick him up at St Pancras.*

Sky: *Party at yours, then, Saturday night?*

Me: *Ha. Ha. I don't think so!*

Sky: *Nah, you probably want to keep him all to yourself.*

Me: *He might be tired. But I promise you'll meet him soon enough. On Sunday, probably. We can all go to the market. Unless they have some group activity arranged.*

Sky: *It's not fair! I want a French exchange student. I wish I went to your school.*

Me: *You're not even doing French GCSE!*

Sky: *Well, I would have done if I'd known I could meet French boys!*

Me: *Sky, you're unbelievable. Anyway, after Rich, I thought you were off boys.*

Sky: *That was ages ago . . . French ones must be better. So, obviously you've got first dibs . . . But if you don't like him, can you save him for me?*

Me: *I might do. Hey, but he might already have a girlfriend. Ever thought of that?*

Sky: *Bummer. Still, he might like a bit of a holiday romance. What happens in Camden stays in Camden. Or something. Or he might have some friends . . .*

Me: *Yeah, well . . . We'll see, OK?*

Sky: *OK. Cool. I wonder what music he's into? Katie's DJing again in a couple of weeks.*

Katie (aka Lady Luscious) is Sky's long-lost sister,

whom she 'found' at one of her long-lost Dad's gigs. It's a long story.

Me: *The French music I've heard is pretty rank. He probably likes accordions.*

Sky: *No!!! Hey – maybe he actually plays an accordion!*

Me: *LOL! Then your mum will love him!*

Sky: *Too true. Although she's only into weird Indian music at the moment.*

Me: *Heh. Lucky you.*

I'm distracted. I can hear Mum moving about downstairs. I look at my watch. It's almost ten-thirty. She'll be needing my help to get upstairs to bed. In that conversation I wasn't supposed to hear, Dad also talked about getting a stairlift installed, but that hasn't happened yet. Mum said it would make her feel like an old granny.

Me: *Sorry, Sky. Better go. Speak tomorrow, OK?*

Sky: *Sure. Night, babes! xxxx*

I log off and go downstairs to see if Mum needs me. She's leaning against the table, her stick in one hand. She looks shattered.

'Did you get all your coursework done?'

'Sure,' I say. 'No worries.' I can finish my English tomorrow, during my free period. 'Want a hand getting up to bed?'

'Actually, I thought I might sleep down here tonight,

on the sofa,' she says, smiling a forced smile. 'If you could just get some bedding out for me and bring me my toothbrush, I'd be really grateful.'

'If you're sure. I don't mind helping you up the stairs . . .'

'No, I'll be better off down here. My balance is hopeless tonight and I don't want us both tumbling down the stairs. I'll be fine for one night. Your dad will be home tomorrow.'

'OK, then.' I don't feel good about this. 'If you're really sure,' I say again.

She nods and perfects her fake smile. I know she hates feeling like a burden. Sometimes I wish I wasn't an only child, so I could talk about these things with someone else. Rosie and Sky are always moaning about their mums. They don't know how lucky they are.

I should have cancelled Xavier. I guess it's too late now.

Chapter 3

Xavier - The Boy from France

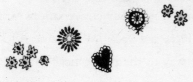

'So,' says Rosie, grinning excitedly. 'Are you ready?'

'Ready as I'll ever be.'

We're standing outside my house, waiting for my dad, who is still loitering by the front door, talking to Rosie's dad about some dull dad-type thing – inflation or investments or house prices. Even Rosie's dad looks bored. We're all about to set off, on foot, to St Pancras station, where the exchange students are coming into London. It's only a mile away and there's nowhere to park, so we'll walk there and get the bus back. Dad can help carry Xavier's suitcase. I'm feeling surprisingly nervous about meeting Xavier, and suddenly worry not just about Mum, but about how I'll entertain him for almost an entire month and whether we'll have anything to talk about. If, that is, we can even manage to talk to each other at all. Why didn't I concentrate more in French class and learn my vocabulary properly? I hope he speaks English, or at least good Franglais (that's a made-up language using half-French, half-English words) because, if I have to speak to him in French, our conversations will consist solely of 'Hello,' 'How are you?' 'What time is it?' and 'Can you tell me the way to the post office?'

Rosie is much more excited about meeting my exchange student than she is about meeting her own. In all our conversations with Sky about their impending visit, I think Manon's name has come up precisely once. Sky and Rosie have it all arranged; apparently, we're all going to be hanging out at my place with Xavier, whether Manon likes it or not. Poor Manon, she hasn't even arrived yet and she's already been relegated to 'tag along' position.

'Right,' says Dad, fastening his coat. At last. 'Shall we go, then? Are you girls ready?'

'We've been ready for about an hour,' says Rosie. She takes her compact out of her bag and applies another coat of lip-gloss. 'Want some?'

I shake my head. I've already let her talk me into applying mascara and concealer and blusher – which I'd normally reserve for a party — because, 'French girls always look groomed.' Anyone would think we're expecting a delegation from Chanel, not some high school in Nice.

'*Allons-y*,' says Dad. That's French for 'Let's go'. He's already showing off his French. When he was a student he spent a year living in Paris and, even though it was over twenty years ago, he still thinks of himself as a local.

I roll my eyes at Rosie and we set off up the road, arm in arm, a few paces behind our dads. It's a cold but sunny day, as good as it gets at this time of year. I'm glad it's not grey and rainy; that would be depressing for someone who comes from a place hot enough for palm trees. I want Xavier's first impression of Camden to be a good one.

St Pancras is left at the top of Royal College Street, just past the old church, with its impressive Victorian tombstones and little park. We're late. We should have set off earlier, but Rosie took ages to get ready and then our dads got caught up in conversation. We enter the station at the opposite side to where we're meeting. I don't mind walking through St Pancras; I like stations, especially this one, with its shops and cafés and hundreds of people from all over the world milling about. There's a buzz of excitement, a pervasive energy, and, even though I'm not travelling anywhere, it's infectious.

I can see them all now, a large group of teenagers and a few adults at the designated meeting point, outside the entrance to the mainline station. As we draw closer, I notice that the remaining French kids are huddled together, waiting to be picked off, one by one, by their English hosts. The boys look clean and smart, with dark jeans, shirts and sweaters, and proper shoes – not like any of the boys I know, who live in trainers and sweatshirts, their tatty jeans halfway down their backsides. The girls are trendier, with ballet pumps, fitted jackets and expertly tied printed scarves. They have a healthy glow about them: tanned skin and glossy, long hair. Almost everybody – girl and boy – is carrying a backpack. Before any of them even open their mouths, you can tell they're tourists.

Dad goes to talk to the exchange programme organisers, while I wait, nervously, at the edge of the group. I watch as people pair off and the crowd depletes. There are lots of English kids I don't recognise – girls from other forms in my year, boys from the local boys' school. I'm not sure where Rosie has gone. I think she said something about finding the loo. She probably wanted to redo her make-up.

Soon there's only one boy left amongst the group of girls. He's tall and dark, and he's wearing brown shoes and a brown leather jacket. He stares at me, hopefully, and, in spite of myself, my tummy does a little flip. This must be Xavier. Just as Sky and Rosie predicted, he's gorgeous. He has a square jaw, green eyes and thick, wavy, dark hair.

'Veecks?' he asks, as I approach.

I nod. 'Um, yes. Hi. You must be Xavier.' I'm trying to act cool, even though my legs feel wobbly. I look around for help from Rosie, but I still can't see her. Dad is deep in conversation with the exchange trip organisers.

Xavier grins. 'Allo.'

'Er, hello. Er, *bonjour*.'

I move to hold out my hand, and he takes it, but he doesn't shake it. Instead, he leans over and kisses me on both cheeks, gently dropping my hand as he does so. He smells like washing powder and hair gel. Mmm. My cheeks glow hot. I take a deep breath and step backwards, hoping he hasn't noticed. 'So, um, did you have a good journey?'

'Yes, no problem, sank you.'

'That's good. Er . . .' Someone rescue me, please; I can't think of a single thing to say. I glance around again for Rosie, and spot her talking to a pretty blond girl, who must be Manon. I try to catch her eye, to beckon them over, but she doesn't see me. 'So, er,' I manage, finally, 'have you been to London before?'

'*Non*. Never. Eez first time. In the moment, I like very much.'

25

I laugh, nervously. He's only seen the train station. 'Cool. Well, we'll go to my house and dump your stuff and then, if you fancy it, we can take a walk around Camden. I'll introduce you to my best friends. Rosie is over there, actually. Although you must be tired. After travelling all day. So maybe you just want to stay in?' I'm rambling now. Still, it's better than saying nothing. 'Anyway, see how you feel. How does that sound?'

'Yes, eez good, sanks.' He looks confused. I was probably talking too fast. He grins again and his eyes crinkle up at the corners, two long dimples appearing in his cheeks. I find myself smiling too, a weird, lopsided smile. My lips are so dry that they're sticking to my teeth. I wish I'd taken Rosie up on her offer of lip-gloss.

'*Bonjour* Xavier, *et bienvenue à Londres!*' says Dad, appearing at my side at last and welcoming Xavier in his best French. I hope he's not going to keep showing off for the entire month. That would be unbearable.

'Allo,' says Xavier. 'You are Veeck's farser? You speak good *Français*.' I wonder if he's going to kiss Dad too, the way I've seen the French boys kissing each other, but he doesn't. They shake hands.

'Yes,' says Dad, looking pleased with himself. 'Call me John. It's a pleasure to meet you, Xavier. Let me take your bags.'

'No, no, eez OK. I can carry my own. Sanks.' He

picks up his enormous duffle bag and sweeps it over his shoulder, as if it's no heavier than a jacket. Dad shrugs. I know he likes to feel useful.

'Right, then,' he says. 'Let's find the others and head home.' He waves Rosie's dad over. Rosie and Manon follow close behind. Rosie grins at me. I catch her looking Xavier up and down and smiling, approvingly.

'Hey, Vix,' she says, putting her arm around my shoulder. She turns to Manon. 'This is Manon. Manon, Vix.'

'Allo,' says Manon. She looks me up and down, the same way Rosie did to Xavier. It makes me feel uncomfortable. 'I stay 'ere wiz Rosie.'

'Hello. This is Xavier. He's staying with me.'

Xavier smiles at me and nods at Manon. 'Allo.'

'Do you two know each other?' asks Rosie.

'*Mais oui,*' says Manon. She leans over to kiss Xavier. 'I know eem a leetle. We go to zee same school in Nice.'

'She eez a very big school,' says Xavier. 'Many students.'

We all stand around, awkwardly, for a few moments, smiling at each other.

'Right,' says Dad. 'Let's go to the bus stop. It's just outside.' He notices that Manon has two wheelie suitcases and offers to take one of them. It's pink and only has a short handle, so he has to bend his knees as he walks. He looks ridiculous.

'We take zee bus now?' says Manon. She seems a little put out. I don't blame her. I guess she's probably tired, after travelling all day.

'Yes, it goes to the end of our street,' Rosie says. 'It's not far. Just five minutes up the road.'

'Ah, all of us go togezzer? You leeve wiz Veecks?'

Rosie laughs. 'Kind of. But no, not in the same house, we're just a few doors down from each other. We've been neighbours – and best friends – since we were little.' She grins at me.

'Ah, OK. Excellent.' Manon glances at Xavier. She seems happy. Xavier, not so much. But perhaps I'm only imagining that.

While we wait for the bus, Rosie chats to me, leaving Xavier and Manon to talk in French. They chatter away ridiculously fast and I can't make out anything they're saying, apart from '*oui*' and '*non*' and '*merci*'. I wonder if they're talking about me or about Rosie.

Rosie leans in towards me. 'I told you he'd be hot,' she whispers. 'And he's hotter than even I expected. Sky is going to be crazy jealous!'

I realise I'm beaming, in spite of myself. It's ridiculous: Xavier and I have barely said two words to each other yet – I know nothing about him. We might not get on. He could be boring. He might even be a French serial killer, for all I know. To tell the truth, I kind of wish he wasn't so good-looking. Every time he smiles at me I go blank. It's the whole accent thing too – it's so cute. 'He is very good-looking,' I concede. 'I'm sure I'll get over it, though. Once I get to know him.'

'Heh,' says Rosie. 'I'm one hundred per cent sure you won't!'

Chapter 4

Fish
and Sheep

Mum is waiting for us by the front door when we
arrive home. She acts as if she's heard us coming
and has only just got here, but I know that she'll really
have been standing here for a while. She has arranged
herself in position, her body balanced against the wall so
she can stand without falling, her stick tucked away, just
out of sight. Whenever she meets someone new she's
embarrassed about her stick, which is silly – and I've told
her – but I guess I'd feel the same. I don't know if
anybody's mentioned to Xavier that she's disabled; maybe
that's what Dad was chatting to the exchange programme
organisers about. I haven't said anything, and I won't, not

unless he asks and I absolutely have to. I know quite a lot about her illness now – too much – because I've been reading about it on the web. I know she's probably going to get worse, but I'm trying not to think about that.

'Hello, Xavier,' says Mum, brightly, as we come in. You'd think she didn't have a worry in the world. Dad takes Xavier's bags straight upstairs. I've made the spare room up for him, as comfortably as I can. I've even put up an old French poster, which I found tucked away behind the bookshelf, to make him feel at home. I hope he likes it.

'Allo, *Madame*,' says Xavier. He leans right over to kiss her, which is good, because it means she doesn't need to take her arm away from the wall and risk losing her balance. '*Enchanté!*'

Mum blushes, just like I did. I don't think I've ever seen her blush before. Xavier's French charm has instantly won her over, too.

'It's lovely to meet you,' she says. 'Please call me Barbara. I hope you had a good journey and that you'll have a wonderful time staying here with us. I know Victoria will look after you. Now please come into the living room and sit down. I'll go and make some tea.'

She waits for us to pass, so that Xavier won't see her picking up her stick, then goes slowly into the kitchen. Dad follows close behind, to help her.

'Victoria? Like zee Queen Victoria?' says Xavier to me,

as we enter the living room. 'I am incorrect? Your name, he ees not Veecks?'

'Vix is really a nickname, a shortening,' I explain, as we sit down on the sofa. 'Only my mum calls me Victoria.'

'Ah. Me too, eef you like, I can call you Victoria?'

'Don't you dare,' I say. 'I hate it. Even most of my teachers call me Vix now.'

'Ah, *oui*?'

'*Oui*. Actually, I thought you were called Ex-avier when I first saw your name. How dumb is that! Now I know your name is pronounced just like xylophone.' As soon as I've said it, I feel like an idiot.

'Zye le Fone? Who is zees? A friend?'

'No, no. Xylophone, the instrument. You know, the one with keys that you hit with sticks.'

'Ah! Gzee–lophone!'

I laugh. 'I do love your accent. It makes everything sound better, somehow.'

He looks crestfallen. 'I have zee axont? I believe I speak zee good Engleesh, wiv zee good axont. You can tell I am *Français*? It is obveeowse?'

'Yes.' I giggle. 'You do have an accent. But don't worry about it — it's cute, very charming. Most people love a French accent, honestly — especially girls.'

He raises an eyebrow. 'Ah, *bon*?'

I look down at the floor, bashfully. I wish I hadn't

mentioned other girls. 'Yes. And I shouldn't laugh, not when your English is so much better than my French.'

'I am sure you speak good *Français*.'

'Nah, I'm rubbish. I'm supposed to practise with you.'

'OK.' He smiles. 'You will learn me better *Anglais* – wiv zee better axont – and I will learn you *Français*.'

'Deal.'

Dad's standing at the door, carrying a tray of tea and biscuits. I don't think we've ever had tea from a teapot, in proper china cups with saucers, before. Usually we have teabags in chipped mugs, with water poured straight from the kettle. What are my parents thinking?

'Have you ever had English tea, Xavier?' says Dad. 'I suppose you're more used to coffee. I used to get a wonderful cup of coffee in a café in the Left Bank. Proper coffee. I remember it well.'

'*Mais oui*, of course. We have tea also.'

Dad sets the tray down on a table. 'Good, good. Shall I be mother?'

I cringe. Xavier appears confused again. I shrug at him and roll my eyes. I think the 'my parents are aliens from another planet' expression translates internationally.

Mum shuffles in with her stick and lowers herself into the armchair. She looks exhausted. I'm sure Xavier must have clocked the stick by now, but he's far too polite to say anything.

'Sank you, Barbara, for your 'ospitalitee,' he says. 'I like very much your 'ome.'

She grins at him. 'It's our pleasure to have you.'

We drink our tea and eat our biscuits and smile at each other a lot, awkwardly. Mum asks Xavier about his journey and Dad talks about his time in Paris. Xavier tries to appear interested, but it turns out that he's only been there once, on a school trip, so he doesn't have much to say about it. I wish Mum and Dad would leave us alone – I'm not used to getting to know someone new in front of my parents; I'm nervous enough as it is.

'So,' says Dad, finally, 'I thought we'd get a takeaway tonight. Save cooking, and it would be nice for Xavier too.'

'Eengleesh food?' says Xavier. 'Cool. I want to try very much.'

'Ah, well, I was actually going to suggest an Indian – which is sort of English food now, you know – or a Chinese.' Dad laughs. 'But we can have something properly English if you prefer. Um, how about fish and chips?'

'Ah *bon*, feesh and sheep?' says Xavier. 'It sounds strange, but I weel try.'

I giggle. 'Not sheep, chips! Fries! Like *frites*. And we can have mushy peas too, if you like,' I say.

'Mooshy pizz? Why not!'

Mum turns her nose up at that idea. 'Poor Xavier,' she says. 'He's come all the way from France, which has the best food in the world, and on his first night we're giving him mushy peas! He's going to think everything they say about British cuisine is true.'

But she's overruled.

Dad goes to fetch the fish and chips from Pang's on Kentish Town Road, which is half a Chinese takeaway and half a fish and chip shop. I've tried fish and chips from several different places in Camden and I like Pang's the best. Dad always enjoys chatting to Mr Pang and, because he likes our family, he always gives us the freshest fish and the newest batch of chips. The portions are enormous. While Dad's gone, I show Xavier around the house, pointing out the kitchen and the bathroom, and checking he has everything he needs. He seems happy with his room, even though it's very bare and a bit girly, with flouncy curtains and a floral bedspread. I hope I haven't forgotten anything.

We hear the front door open. 'Fish and chips!' calls Dad, from downstairs. 'Come and get it!'

'Come on,' I say to Xavier. He holds the bedroom door open for me and lets me through first. None of the English boys I know would ever do that.

We eat at the kitchen table. I prefer to eat fish and chips straight out the wrapping, but Mum insists on plates. Xavier watches curiously as I drench my chips in vinegar, then does the same. He tries a chip. 'Mmm,' he says. Next he takes a forkful of his fish. 'Mmm,' he says again. 'Feesh and sheep eez gude!' he declares. He tries the peas, tentatively. They're luminous green and very runny, which must be a little off-putting. He pushes them around his plate with his fork.

'And how do you like your mushy peas?' I say.

He makes a funny expression, a sort of furrowed-eyebrow, pouty sneer, which makes him look particularly French. 'Um, they are gude also, I sink.'

I laugh. 'They're an acquired taste. You don't have to eat them, honestly. Don't worry.'

He polishes off the lot anyway. And when he notices that I've left some of my chips, he helps himself to those too.

'That's what I like to see,' says Dad. 'A hearty appetite!'

Throughout the meal my phone has been beeping constantly. I don't need to look at it to know that I'll have messages from Sky and Rosie, wanting to know how things are going with Xavier. Mum asks me to turn my phone off but, instead, I put it on silent and, when nobody's looking, check it quickly under the table.

Rosie says Xavier is v hot! x reads Sky's first text.

How r u getting on? x reads Rosie's.

A few minutes later: *Wot r u doing? Tl me! Sx*

And then: *Vix txt me! Rx*

Vix! Gt back 2 me!!! Sx

I say I'm going to the loo and quickly text them back, telling them things are going well and that I'll talk to them properly later, when I'm alone. I wonder how Rosie is getting on with Manon.

After dinner, I do the washing up and Xavier offers to help, probably because he doesn't want to sit making polite conversation with my parents and hearing more about Dad's amazing year in France (which happened aeons before Xavier was born). Then I ask if it's OK for us to go upstairs to my room. Some parents have rules about having boys in your bedroom; mine don't because I've never had a boyfriend. They say it's fine.

Xavier walks around my room, studying my posters and the photos of my friends, which I've made into a framed montage and put up by the bed. He asks me who everybody is, and how I know them all. He appears genuinely interested. I have to repeat myself a couple of times, explain a few phrases, but his English really is pretty good.

Then I ask him all about his life. Like most people in Nice, he lives in an apartment, not a house, with his mum, dad and two sisters. It's about five minutes from the port in Nice and only ten minutes from the beach. He and his friends seem to spend much of their time there – after school, at weekends, at beach parties in the summer. It's an outdoor life, filled with swimming and cycling and skateboarding, playing football, camping in the woods, enjoying barbecues and campfires. No wonder he looks so tanned and healthy. And fit. But I'm not thinking about *that*. We're just talking, getting to know each other, making friends. To tell the truth, I feel quite jealous of his lifestyle and I wonder if he's going to find Camden boring, especially now it's getting colder, and picnicking on Primrose Hill or hanging out in Regent's Park are probably out. I've never questioned it before, but my life is mostly lived indoors: sitting in coffee shops, lounging around at friends' houses, chatting in my bedroom. And, while he seems to hang out with equal numbers of boys and girls, almost all of my friends are girls: Rosie, Sky and a few assorted girls from school, or those I know through my family. My only real male friend is Max, Rosie's ex, and he doesn't live in London.

I try to make my life sound more exciting, though. I tell him about the market, about local gigs I've been to, the art collective on my street where – according to rumour – the artist Winksy is said to live, and the fact that I know the drummer from supergroup, Fieldstar, who lives a few doors down. I make out that my life is one big, celebrity-filled party when, really, I go to school, see my mates and help look after my mum. Somehow, I feel like I need to show off to him when, usually, I'm happy just being myself. I don't know why. It's stupid.

But it works; he seems impressed. 'You are so lucky to leeve in Camden Town,' he says. 'I have always dreamed to veesit her. We can go to see it all, soon?'

'Sure, we can go to the market tomorrow, if you like. With Rosie, who you met earlier, and Sky, the one I showed you in the pictures. She's dying to meet you.'

'Cool. I hear so much about zis place.'

'And Manon, she'll come too. So you'll have someone French to talk to.'

'Ah, OK,' he says, not very enthusiastically. Maybe he doesn't want to hang around with other French people. '*Bon*. And your boyfriend, he comes too?'

'I don't have a boyfriend,' I say. I pause. 'Not at the moment, anyway.'

He smiles. 'Ah, *bon?*'

'Yeah. What about you? Er, do you have a girlfriend?' I'm almost certain he's going to say yes. Some lucky French girl must have snapped him up.

'*Non*. How you say? No one special at zis time.'

'Oh,' I say, trying not to sound too pleased. As if he'd be interested in me. 'Well, maybe you'll meet someone here. One of my friends, perhaps.'

'Maybe.'

'Anyway, it's late. You must be knackered. I should let you get some sleep.'

'Nackaired?'

I giggle. 'Tired. Exhausted. Like a horse that's not fit for anything any more and gets sent to the . . . never mind.'

'I am like zee horse?'

'No, no. It just means really tired. It's kind of slang.' Talking to someone who doesn't speak English as their first language is difficult; it's really making me think about the words I use every day and never question.

'Ah *bon*. Yes, I am vairee tired. I sleep and tomorrow we go to zee market, *oui*?'

'*Oui!*'

'Sank you, Veecks. *A demain*.'

I think that means until tomorrow. I smile. 'Yeah, see you tomorrow. Let me know if you need anything. Goodnight Xavier.'

'*Bonne nuit*. Gude night.' He leans over to kiss me again. I'm not sure if I'm supposed to kiss him back, so I blow little kisses into the air. He doesn't smell quite so fresh any more, after the fish and chips – more like vinegar, now – but I don't mind. I don't mind at all.

I leave Xavier to get ready for bed and go into my bedroom, so I can log in online and tell Rosie and Sky all about him. I realise I'm smiling, that I feel warm and tingly inside, a little hyper, even. Maybe they put something in the mushy peas, because I really can't think why.

Chapter 5
Croissants and Hot Chocolate

I wake in a bouncy mood. It's another sunny day — perfect for a visit to the market. I leap out of bed and then, as quickly as I can, take a shower, get dressed and drag a brush through my hair. I wouldn't normally do all that — not before breakfast on a Sunday — but I know I wouldn't feel comfortable wandering around in my dressing gown in front of Xavier. I think he's still asleep (at least there doesn't seem to be any light or sound from his room) so I go downstairs to talk to Mum and Dad. Mum is sitting in the armchair, apparently reading the paper, but it doesn't look like she's able to concentrate. She looks up at me and smiles.

'Did you sleep well?'

'I slept great, thanks. Did you?'

'Not too bad. A bit restless.' She grimaces. Something must hurt, somewhere. It could be anywhere on her body – her face, her arms, her legs. She's told me the pain is a bit like having lots of tiny electric shocks, which sounds horrible. Normal painkillers can't touch it, so the doctor has given her these heavy-duty pills, which she doesn't like taking because they make her feel woozy and down.

'Are you in pain, Mum?' I say. 'Can I get you anything? A hot water bottle, maybe?'

'I'll be OK.' She smiles, bravely. 'It's not too bad. Anyway, I'd rather feel something than nothing. My legs are almost completely numb now. I trod on a pin yesterday; it went right through my shoe and I didn't notice!'

'Ouch.' I screw up my face. I don't know what else to say. Last month, she picked up a pan from the hob and badly burned her hand because she couldn't feel how hot the handle was. It really makes me worry. 'I'm going to make a cup of tea. Want one?'

'No, thanks. Is Xavier up yet? Dad's been to Sainsbury's and bought croissants for him.'

'Cool. No, Xavier's still asleep, I think. Did he get the chocolate ones?'

'You'll have to have a look in the kitchen. Dad's doing

some work in the garage, I think.' She puts the paper down on the coffee table. It's crumpled, as if she's been gripping it too long in the same place. Maybe she found it hard to turn the page. 'Xavier seems very nice, doesn't he?'

'Yes,' I say, my cheeks pinkening. Why does that happen every time I think about him? 'I hope it's going to be all right for you, having him here for a whole month.'

'He doesn't seem like he's going to be any trouble,' says Mum. She appears relieved, as if she feared he might have been. 'He seems well brought-up, mature for his age.'

'Yes, I guess he is. I'm going to take him to the market today, with Sky and Rosie. What are you going to do?'

'Well . . .' She pauses. 'I thought I might run a marathon and then go to my tap-dancing class, if the ice rink is closed.'

'Great,' I say, playing along. We both know that she'll be spending the day at home, in the living room. But Mum always says that if you can't laugh about your problems, you'd lose it completely and might as well give up altogether. She says black humour is the best medicine. 'That's a bit lazy, though. You might want to add in a cycle ride, to Brighton, maybe.'

'After lunch,' she says. 'And tonight I'm going ballroom dancing.'

'Make sure you wear your six-inch heels.'

'Naturally.'

I can hear movement upstairs. Xavier must be awake. I clamber up from the sofa and check out my reflection in the living-room mirror; I look OK, I think. Now I can hear him coming down the stairs. I lean against the bookshelf, holding my breath.

There's a knock on the door. 'Allo? Veecks?' I open it. Xavier looks sleepy, his eyes still half closed and his hair sticking out in all directions. It's cute. I have this urge to ruffle it. Oh my God! What is wrong with me?

I compose myself. 'Morning, Xavier. Did you sleep OK? Would you like some tea and croissants?'

'Wunderfool. Sanks.'

'Come on then,' I say, leaving Mum and gesturing to Xavier to follow me into the kitchen. 'I love croissants, don't you? I guess they're not much of a novelty for you, though. Don't you have croissants for breakfast every day?'

'*Non*, I have zee cereal or baguette wiz zee, how you say? *Confiture*, er, jam. We have zee croissants on Sundays, wiz hot chocolah.'

'Really? With hot chocolate? Mmm, that sounds good. Do you want me to make some of that instead?'

'*Oui*, if you 'ave some. I would like very much.'

I reach into the cupboard and pull out the jar of cocoa. Xavier watches me, rubbing his eyes, as I boil up the milk and add the sugar and cocoa powder. Soon, we each have a mug of thick, steaming hot chocolate. It smells so good I can taste it before I even try it. 'Sit down,' I say, handing him the bag of croissants. 'Have as many as you like.'

'*Merci*, Veecks.' He tears off a chunk of croissant and dunks it into his hot chocolate, swirling it around to pick up as much of the rich, sweet liquid as he can. Then he puts the whole lot in his mouth at once, swallows and licks his lips. There's still a big blob of chocolate on his chin, but I don't like to tell him.

'*C'est magnifique!*' he says. I think that means he likes it. 'Now you try.'

'OK . . .' He watches, grinning, as I break off a small piece of my croissant and tentatively dip it into my mug. I taste it. It's delicious. 'Mmm, that's yummy!' This is one French custom I'm definitely going to adopt. Even though I dread to think how many calories there are in it. And yet, none of the French kids I saw at the station was fat.

'*Oui!*' he says. 'Miam miam!' I guess that means yummy. 'Now you must 'ave some more. Don't be so delicate.'

When we've finished our hot chocolate, Xavier picks up the last croissant and breaks it in two. 'We share,' he says. He uses his half to wipe his mug clean of any last chocolate traces. So, because it's only polite, I do the same.

'*Voilà!*' he says, as if I've done something very good, and beams at me.

I check my watch. We're meeting Rosie and the others in half an hour. 'Thanks for that, Xavier. You should go and get ready now. I'll do the washing up.'

It only takes him ten minutes to shower and get dressed. When he comes back downstairs, wearing a clean sweater and jeans, his hair is still damp and he has that yummy, fresh, soapy smell again.

He frowns at me. 'Veecks, why did you not tell me I 'ad zee chocolah on my, 'ow you say, cheen?'

I laugh. 'Sorry.'

'No problem.' His eyes twinkle, mischievously. 'By zee way, you also have zee chocolah. Zare.' He points to the corner of my mouth, licks his finger and, before I'm aware what's happening, he's rubbing the side of my mouth clean. My stomach lurches so hard it must be audible. This is not something I would ever dream of doing to someone I'd just met. It's so . . . familiar. And yet, in a weird way, so lovely too.

'Zare,' he says, looking distinctly pleased with himself. 'All gone.'

As are all the thoughts in my head.

Chapter 6

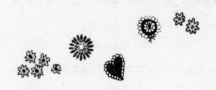

Chemistry

amden Market is like any other shopping street to me and to my friends, Rosie and Sky. We come here almost every weekend and could now find our way through the maze of stalls with our eyes closed. But to someone who's never been here before, especially a tourist, Camden Market is a place of wonder – a sort of alternative theme park. I love seeing it through a stranger's eyes, as they take it all in: the weirdly dressed people, the smells emanating from the food outlets, the music, bright colours and general mayhem. I'm excited to see what Xavier will make of it.

We've arranged to meet Rosie and Manon and Sky

by the bridge at the Lock in half an hour. Xavier wants to buy some London souvenirs for his family, so on the way I take him to one of those tacky tourist shops on Camden High Street that sell everything you never dreamed you needed (and don't), all adorned with pictures of red telephone boxes, red buses or the London skyline. He chooses a London bus keyring for his dad and a set of fridge magnets for his mum. The red paint is already flaking off the keyring.

'Now I am a real Camden guy,' he says, putting his Union Jack emblazoned plastic bag into his rucksack. He looks so happy that I don't want to disillusion him by telling him that nobody who actually lives in London would buy any of these things . . . not in a million years.

'Yes, I'm sure your family will love them.'

'London is just as I imagined. Except no fog. About zis, I am disappointed.'

'Sorry?'

'The weather, it is cold but sunny. Since I arrive, no rain, no fog. I want to see London fog. Like in zee movies. Like in Sherlock 'olmes.'

I giggle. 'That was in Victorian times. It isn't foggy in London any more, not that I've noticed.'

He pouts, for comic effect. 'No fog? *Bof*.'

'*Bof*?'

'*Oui, bof*! Eez difficult to translate. Like, erm, nevair

mind, I don't care, in a way. But not. Just *bof*!'

'Ah, you mean like . . . meh?'

'Meh?'

'Yes, meh.' I laugh. This is a ridiculous conversation. 'And, er, *bof*. I think we're lost in translation. Come on, the others will be waiting.'

Camden Lock is so busy today that it's hard to find my friends. And part of me hopes that I won't, because it would be great to show Xavier my favourite areas of the market without having to please anybody else. Eventually, we spot them loitering by a stall that sells handmade silver jewellery. Manon drops the bracelet she's handling and makes a beeline for Xavier, virtually pushing me out of the way to greet him. She gives him three – not two – kisses on his cheek and then starts chattering away in French so fast that I can't make out a single word. I stand there like an English spare part for a minute, then decide to leave them to it and go over to join Rosie and Sky. As we embrace, I can't help noticing that Rosie is wearing a green polka-dot silk scarf, which I've never seen before, tied in a complicated knot.

'New scarf?'

Rosie grins, proudly. 'It's Manon's. She lent it to me and showed me loads of ways to tie it. Do you like it?'

'Yes, it suits you.'

'I might look for something similar in the market.

Something vintage, maybe, to go with my other jacket.'

'Good idea. So how is Manon? Are you getting on OK?'

'Manon's really cool, thank God,' says Rosie. 'We had a real laugh, last night, trying on each other's clothes and stuff. I think she's going to fit right in.'

'Yeah, she seems nice,' says Sky. 'I chatted to her on the way up here.'

'That's good,' I say, conscious that Manon hasn't been very friendly to me so far, at least. 'Maybe I'll talk to her later and get to know her a little better.'

Rosie smiles. 'You should. She's going to be in our class at school too, so we'll be spending loads of time with her.'

'Great,' I say. It doesn't come out as enthusiastically as it should have done. 'How's her English?'

'Really good. Miles better than my French.'

'Yeah, Xavier's is too. It's embarrassing. Why are they so much better than us?'

'I guess they hear English all the time, in films and music, so it's easier to pick it up. We only do French at school.'

'Good point. Don't you love their accent though?'

'Yeah. It's super cute.'

I tell Sky and Rosie about the 'fish and sheep' and they laugh. Maybe not as hard as I would like, but perhaps you had to be there.

'Sounds like you're having fun with Xavier,' says Sky, with a knowing smile. 'And he is just as fit as Rosie said. So . . . are you going to introduce me then? Don't worry, I know you've got first option.'

'Ha ha. Course. Sorry, I forgot you haven't met him yet. Come on.'

I take her arm and steer her over to Xavier and Manon. They're still talking at a million miles an hour, with no apparent gaps between their sentences or breaths between their words. I'm about to interrupt when Xavier spots me, stops speaking, and turns to me and grins, like he's really pleased I'm there. Manon seems nonplussed.

'Xavier, this is Sky,' I say. 'Sky, this is Xavier. I think you've already met Manon.'

'*Enchanté,*' he says, kissing Sky. 'Your name eez Sky? Like *le ciel*?'

Sky laughs and shoots me a bemused glance. 'If you say so.'

'Sky can't speak any French at all,' I explain, thankful I understand what he's just said. Lucky I was paying attention in the weather vocabulary lesson a few years back. 'Yes, like the sky. Her mum is a sort of hippy.'

'Cool,' says Xavier.

Sky shakes her head. 'Not really. It's a pain in the . . . really annoying most of the time.'

Rosie sidles over. 'Come on, guys. We really should

look around the market, if we're going to.'

And that's exactly what we do, for the next hour or so. We check out T-shirt stalls and poster stalls, stalls selling incense and perfumes, home-made cakes, candles and jewellery, and cavernous spaces where you can buy musical instruments, second-hand clothes and furniture. We take each other's photos standing by the giant bronze horse statues in the Stables Market, drink orange juice freshly squeezed in front of us, and try on dresses in a vintage boutique (all except for Xavier, obviously). Rosie has an Indian head massage, which makes her giggle, and frizzes her hair, and Manon buys a tan leather handbag. I tell her I like it and she says, 'Of course,' which I think is a bit rude. Maybe it's a language thing.

Now Sky is suggesting we might like to stop to have an ice cream.

'Good plan,' I say. It's not strictly ice-cream weather (about ten degrees too cold), but I know why Sky has come up with this idea. We're standing just a few metres from the entrance to the weirdest ice-cream parlour in Camden. In London. Or, in the world, probably. It's called The Chin Chin Laboratorists (I have no idea why) and it's like a cross between a GCSE science lab and an ice-cream shop. The staff wear white lab coats and safety goggles and they use test tubes and beakers filled with colourful solutions. They make the ice cream right in front of you, using liquid nitrogen, producing huge clouds of white gas. Don't ask me how, but it creates the creamiest ice cream. And even though there are only a few flavours to choose from each day, they're the most imaginative flavours you could dream up: birthday cake, mango and pepper, hot cross buns and Earl Grey tea or basil choc chip. There are tons of yummy toppings too. It's all very Willy Wonka. You can even play on swings outside. I wonder what our French guests will make of it.

Sky gathers everyone together. 'Ice cream?' she says, to no one in particular.

Rosie nods, enthusiastically, as do I. But Manon scrunches up her nose and pouts, in exactly the way Xavier does when he's not sure about something. When he makes that face, it's cute; I think it makes her look arrogant. 'No, no,' she says. 'Eez too cold. And I eat too much already. Coffee, instead, maybe?'

'Xavier? What about you?' I say, disregarding her. (Well, she's been practically ignoring me all day.) I already know how much Xavier likes his food; I don't think he'll take much persuading. 'This isn't normal ice cream. It's like nothing you've seen or tasted before. You've got to try it.'

'Yes . . . OK,' he says. 'Eez cold, but I try.'

I lead him into the ice cream parlour, with the others following close behind. His eyes light up as he takes in the spectacle and grow even wider as the ice cream maker – or chemist – creates his chocolate ice cream in front of him, explaining each step of the process. He's almost too excited to choose a topping, so I pick sugar-coated frogs' legs (not real) for him (as a little joke). Rosie has chocolate too, with a sea-salted caramel topping, while Sky and I decide to be adventurous and try the blueberry muffin flavour. It's insanely tasty.

Manon looks on, grumpily, taking delicate sips of her coffee as we enjoy our ice creams. I think she's too proud to change her mind and have one. I wish she wasn't here. I rarely dislike anybody, especially when I first meet them, but there's something about her that grates on me. Still, I must try to hide my feelings. Rosie seems to like her a lot, and she's going to be around for a few weeks. Maybe I just need to try harder.

No time like the present. 'Hey, Manon,' I say, brightly. 'So what do you think of Camden Market?'

'I like,' she says, without looking up from her coffee. That's it. Then she turns to Xavier and starts gabbling to him in French.

I glance over at Sky and raise my eyebrows. She smiles back at me, sweetly. So she hasn't noticed how 'off' Manon is being with me? Surely I'm not imagining it? Or could there be another explanation? Could I be . . . jealous? It's not a feeling I recognise. Or one that I like.

And it's irrational: Xavier isn't my boyfriend, or anywhere near it. He's just a guy who's randomly staying in my house. We're getting on really well, but I've known him for less than twenty-four hours. So why do I feel so anxious and annoyed every time he talks to Manon?

Chapter 7

Amy's House

'Are you OK, Xavier?' I can't help noticing that he seems bored. Not in a rude, huffing and puffing way – he's trotting around with us, patiently waiting while we try on clothes and jewellery – but I can tell that he's not really enjoying himself any more. I don't think boys *get* shopping, especially clothes shopping, not unless they need to buy something.

'Of course,' he says. 'No problem.'

'It's just . . . I mean, would you rather go somewhere else? I guess it must be a bit rubbish for you, hanging out with girls all day, looking at dresses and stuff. Even I get bored sometimes.'

He shrugs. 'No, zees is not a problem. I have seesters. It's nor-mal.'

'But there must be something you'd like to see. Something you'd prefer to do? Isn't there?'

He hesitates for a moment, as if he's not sure whether I'm serious, then smiles. 'Er, Veecks, do you know what it eez zat I would like very much to do?'

I don't know, I think, gazing at his dimples. *Kiss me?*

Oh my goodness! Where did that come from? That crazy thought has popped into my mind from absolutely nowhere and, try as I might, I can't get it out. I jerk my head, as though it will help to dislodge the idea and stop my cheeks from burning up. Of course that's not what he's going to say. As if! Here, in the middle of the market, with all our friends around us and, more to the point, when he doesn't fancy me anyway? He's more likely to say 'rob a bank'.

'I . . . don't . . . know,' I say, hesitantly. 'Tell me . . .' I wait, not daring to breathe, just in case a genie suddenly decides to leap out of a nearby fairy tale and grant my wish. As they do.

'I'd like to go to zee 'ouse of zee singair, Amy Wine'ouse. She leeved in Camden, no?'

My fantasy genie evaporates. 'Oh, OK, right, sure. Yes, she did.' I know it's stupid, but I can't help but sound disappointed. I clear my throat. 'OK, cool. I can show you where it is.'

He smiles. 'Excellont. Zis is what I want to see most in all of Camden Town.'

'Really? I'm surprised. So you're a fan, then?'

'Ah, *oui*. I love Amy Wine'ouse.'

'Yeah? I didn't know she was big in France. Me too. I'm a huge fan.' This is the truth, although I can't help thinking that I'd probably have said it anyway, just to please him. Which means I'm officially turning into the sort of girl I claim to hate. 'Actually, I used to see her around Camden sometimes. She seemed nice, friendly.'

'Wow! You knew Amy Wine'ouse!' He glances around him, expectantly, as if he's about to announce this exciting news to everybody else. Luckily, they're all out of earshot.

'Not exactly,' I say. 'Kind of. Sort of. A bit. We weren't exactly friends. Just neighbours. Distant neighbours. Anyway . . .'

He grins. 'Then we go now? Eet's OK? Eet's far from 'ere?'

'Not too far. Hold on. Let me tell my friends.' I look around for the others. Sky is rifling through a box of vinyl, probably so she can buy something for her DJ half-sister. Rosie and Manon have ventured a little further into the stalls and appear to be showing each other some plaited leather belts. I hesitate. I should probably ask them if they want to join us. But Rosie won't want to come,

I'm sure of it. She's already told me that she doesn't see the point of hanging around outside a dead singer's house when there's a live rock star living right next door (the drummer from Fieldstar, to be precise, but that's a whole other story). Not to mention that she's been to visit about a hundred times already. I really don't want her to bring Manon, who has still barely said a word to me. More to the point, I'm entitled to some alone time with Xavier, aren't I?

I walk up behind Sky and playfully put my hands on her shoulders, making her jump. 'Only me,' I tell her. 'Listen, Xavier's had enough. You know. So I'm going to take him home. Is that OK with you?'

'Sure,' says Sky. 'There's a few things I want to check out, so I won't come back with you now, if that's OK. We'll catch up later, yeah?'

'Course. Um, Rosie and Manon look busy. I don't want to interrupt them. Will you tell them for me?'

'No worries.' She hugs me and flashes me a coy little smile. 'Have fun with Xavier.'

'We're just going home,' I say, flushing. Can she tell how I feel about him? Is it that obvious? 'We'll probably end up sitting talking to Mum and Dad or something. Boring. Anyhow, see you later.'

I turn away before she can say anything else and walk back over to Xavier.

He smiles. 'Your friends? Don't they come also?'

'Er, nobody else really fancies it,' I say, leaving out the part that I didn't give them a choice. If anyone objects later, I can always say we thought of the Amy Winehouse idea on the way home and took a detour.

'No problem.'

It's probably wishful thinking, but he doesn't seem the slightest bit unhappy about this.

We head back up the high street and take a shortcut through Sainsbury's on to Camden Road. Well, it's meant to be a shortcut, except Xavier seems fascinated by the prospect of checking out an English supermarket, and asks if we can wander the aisles for a few minutes. I agree, to humour him, although frankly it seems a bit weird. Who goes food shopping for fun? Especially a boy. And who prefers Sainsbury's to Camden Market? He says he wants to see what food you can buy in England, whether it's the same as in French supermarkets, and whether (I'm guessing, because he's too polite to say it) English food is as rubbish as French people think. So I follow him around, letting him peer into the freezer cabinets and pick up and replace things from the shelves until he's satisfied.

'Zee food 'ere. Eez the same, almost,' he declares, appearing disappointed. 'One can even buy zee baguettes and zee Camembert.'

'Course,' I say. 'It's England, not a third-world country.

We have everything. We don't live on fish and chips and roast beef. No frogs' legs or snails here, though, I'm afraid.' I'm aware I sound a bit miffed. Xavier doesn't know how much time I spend trudging around here, buying stuff for Mum, when I'd rather be doing something else. It's not my favourite place. I force a smile. 'Come on, I thought you wanted to see Amy's house.'

'But yes,' he says. 'Of course. Let us go. But one day, we come back and buy zee food and I'll cook for you and your family, a proper French dinair. If it pleases you.'

'I would like that,' I say, surprised. 'You cook? Seriously?'

'*Oui*, my mother, she teaches me.'

He doesn't seem the slightest bit embarrassed by this. He even seems proud. I don't know any boys who cook. Not one. The boys I know think the only food worth eating comes out of polystyrene cartons with a logo stamped on them. Cooking is for girls and wusses. But Xavier is most definitely not a wuss.

'Do all boys cook in France? Everyone here just goes to McDonald's or KFC.'

'No, I don't sink so. My friends, they prefer McDonald also. I like too, sometimes. But I enjoy to cook.'

'Cool.' I blush. I think he might just be the perfect boy. 'Well, Amy's house is about ten minutes up Camden Road, just off it, in a posh little square.'

'A leetle scware?' He looks perplexed. Maybe they don't have squares in France, or maybe he can't pronounce it.

'Yeah, like a street with a green bit in the middle . . . Never mind. You'll see.'

We stroll up Camden Road, chatting about his sisters; he has two, both older than him, one of whom has left home already and is training as a teacher in Paris. I tell him they sound cool and he makes that raised eyebrow, half-frown, half-pout expression again, which makes him look so very French. I don't tell him that I've always wanted a sister, someone to chat to and share things with, especially when things get hard with Mum. Even a brother would do. Being an only child sucks sometimes. Maybe that's why I'm so close to Rosie and Sky; I guess I think of them as my surrogate sisters.

'So what else do you like doing in Nice, apart from going to the beach?' I ask.

'I play volleyball and football.'

'Yeah? Are you any good?'

'Not bad. I am in zee school team.'

'Cool. I used to play football too, when I was younger. I play netball now – I'm top scorer in my year, actually.'

'Ah, *oui*? Netball?'

'You don't have it? It's like basketball, I guess, except you don't bounce the ball.'

He stops and looks me up and down, then grins. 'But you are not so tall.'

I redden. I'm a perfectly average height, I just feel awkward when he stares at me. 'You don't have to be for netball.'

'Ah, *oui?*'

'Wee.' It's practically the first French word I've said since he arrived and I feel ridiculously self-conscious about my accent. I know the whole point of the exchange is to improve my French speaking but Xavier is so good at English, and his accent is so appealing when he speaks it, that there isn't much incentive to try.

He smiles. 'Ah, *tu parles Français!*'

'Yes,' I say. 'I can speak a tiny bit of French but your English is tons better. And my accent is awful.'

'No! Eez cute axont. I love zee axont *Anglais.*'

'Really?' I've never really considered that French people might like English accents as much as we like French ones. It's hard to imagine that my North London vowels can sound sexy to anyone.

He nods and I blush for what must be the millionth time today. 'Come on,' I say, changing the subject. 'We're nearly there. We just need to cross the road.'

Before I can stop him, he has stepped off the kerb. A motorbike zooms past, missing him by a nose. On instinct, I grab his jacket and drag him back to safety. 'Xavier, what are you thinking? Don't they teach you the Green Cross Code in France?'

'*Mon dieu!*' he says, appearing visibly shaken. 'My God! I sink I was looking zee wrong way. I forget – you Engleesh drive on zee left.'

'Er, yes, we do. It's kind of an important thing to remember. God, Xavier, please don't do that again. Apart from anything else, can you imagine how much trouble I'll be in if I get you run over?'

He laughs. 'No worries. I am *Français*. I cannot be hurt by zee English cars.'

'It wasn't a car, it was a motorbike. Quite a cool one, actually.'

'Ah, *oui*. You like zee motorbikes?'

'God, yes. I'm not allowed to ride one yet, obviously. But I've always wanted a motorbike and as soon as I'm old enough, I'm going to get one. Or a scooter, at least.'

He seems impressed, like boys always are. But this is one guy whom I really don't want seeing me as 'one of the lads'. Well done, Vix, I tell myself, you've done it again.

Or maybe not . . .

'My cousin, he has a scooter. He lets me ride it sometimes, not on zee roads. Maybe if you come to Nice I can give you a ride, on zee back.'

Is he inviting me to Nice? That means he likes me and wants to stay in touch. Or maybe I'm reading too much into a throwaway comment . . . 'Cool,' I say, turning away, so he can't see blush one million and one. 'Come on. It's safe to cross now.'

We walk a short way further up Camden Road and then turn right into a little road, which leads into Camden Square. 'This is it,' I say, stopping to allow him to take it in. I think he'll probably be disappointed: it's just a square of large, expensive townhouses, with some greenery in the middle. Just another Camden street. A pretty street but, in the end, only a street. There's nothing much to see any more. For weeks, months, after she died, the place was like a shrine, with hordes of fans pouring through, singing and crying together and leaving photographs and mementos. But the tributes to Amy – the bottles, bouquets, photos, candles and notes – have long since been removed, leaving just the street sign covered in her fans' scrawlings and some RIP messages carved into the trees. It doesn't stop people coming though; tourists are always stopping me in Camden Road to ask the way to Amy's house. When I give them directions, they look at me with respect, as if I'm privileged to be a real Camdener.

Xavier gazes around. He's quiet, mournful, like somebody in church. 'Which eez zee 'ouse of Amy?' he asks, eventually.

'It's at the end,' I say, pointing to the far corner. 'You

can't get right up to it, but I'll take you as far as we can go.'

I lead him across the square until we're a respectful distance from the house. 'It's that one,' I say, looking up. He looks up too, at the tall Edwardian villa, and nods. He doesn't say anything. I guess, like everybody else who comes to visit, he's imagining what it was like to live and die in there.

We stand in silence for a minute or two and then he takes my hand and gives me a little hug. 'Sank you, Veecks,' he says, into my collar. 'For taking me to zees place.'

I hug him back, my heart pounding wildly, my nose pressed into his neck. As I breathe in his scent, I think that I'd be happy staying like this all day – hell, for the rest of my life if I could. And then the moment is gone and I start to feel awkward and self-conscious. I can't tell if he's simply feeling emotional, and just wants to hug someone, and I'm the only person around, or if he really does want to hug *me*. Realising that I'm enjoying the hug a little too much, and that it probably doesn't mean what I want it to mean, I pull away.

'Come on,' I say. 'Let's go home. We can play some Amy tracks later if you like.'

Chapter 8
A Little White Lie

Mum hasn't always been ill, although I can't remember a time when she wasn't. She told me that it all started just after I was born. One day, when I was tiny – about a month old – her left eye went all blurry, and she couldn't see properly for about a week. She thought it was just because she was so tired from getting up in the night to feed me. It made sense. I was a bit of a nightmare as a baby, everyone says – always crying, never sleeping. Her eye got better all by itself and then, a couple of months later, she woke up one morning, tried to get out of bed, and discovered that her legs simply wouldn't work. She says they felt like wads of cotton wool crumpling beneath her. She ended up falling on to the carpet and lying there, helpless, until Dad came back from the shops and heard her calling out. I was in my cot at the end of the bed and I was screaming and screaming because I was hungry and needed my nappy changing, but there was nothing she could do. It must have been really scary for her.

Months passed and her legs got better too but, after that, she was never the same again. Her symptoms came and went. Sometimes her hands wouldn't work properly, sometimes it was her legs or her eyes. She says she felt exhausted all the time. There she was, a new mum with a tiny baby, and some days she couldn't even walk or carry me. She saw all kinds of doctors and had tons of horrible tests, and it took months to find out what was wrong. There wasn't a cure.

For a few years, when I was little, she was fairly well, and so I guess I got used to having a 'normal' mum, who could take me out to the park and play with me and pick me up from my friends' houses. I was too young to remember what had happened when I was a baby so, when she was too tired to do anything with me, I didn't understand. When she said she had a bad leg or pain in her arms, it didn't make sense; she hadn't had an accident, had she? Sometimes, I thought she was angry with me because I'd been naughty, or maybe she was avoiding me because she didn't love me very much.

And then, when I was ten, her legs turned to cotton wool again and, this time, they didn't get better. She stumbled around, falling into things, until she gave in and had to start using a stick. That's when my parents finally told me what was wrong: something called multiple sclerosis, or MS for short. Now, the doctors say her illness is progressing. She's never going to get better, only worse.

I've asked her about it many times because I can't help feeling guilty. Maybe if she hadn't given birth to me, she would have stayed well. Maybe it's my fault. She swears that it isn't and that, even if it was, she would still have had me. Her illness had probably been lying dormant in her brain for years, waiting for an opportunity to pounce. I've read a lot about it on the internet – secretly, because Mum and Dad say that there's too much scary information out there, which I don't need to worry about – and it says that some women with her illness do have their first symptoms, or get worse, after they have a baby. Whatever she says, I can't help blaming myself.

Maybe that's why I feel so confused and annoyed with myself when I resent having to do things for her. I tell everybody that I don't mind, and they all think I'm so mature and sensible and responsible. But I do mind. I really do. The only thing Rosie and Sky ever have to do is clean their own bedrooms or, if they're really unlucky, help with the washing up. I'd love to have all the free time that they have to instant message, text and go on Facebook, fool around with make-up, or just lie in late at the weekends. The only way I fit everything in is by being super organised. I'd love to be able to go out with them and not be worrying about how Mum is, and what I'll have to do when I get home. I'd love to have some time just for me. I don't say anything because I don't want to seem ungrateful or be a moaner. Nobody really understands unless they've been there, do they? I don't want to be different. I don't want people to feel sorry for me. I want to be like everybody else.

And that's why, after thinking about it, I've decided not to tell Xavier what's wrong with my mum. If he asks, I'm going to tell him she had an accident and hurt her leg. A car accident, maybe, if he wants more details. It's only a little white lie. What harm can it do?

Chapter 9
Cheesy Yogurt

Monday morning. Bleuggh. At least Dad is here, so I don't have to help Mum before school today. But I can't get up yet – it would be against the laws of nature; my bed feels so cosy and my duvet fits my body so well, as if it was made to measure. Maybe if I just let my eyelids flutter shut for a few more minutes . . .

And there's that horrible alarm again, piercing through my dreams. OK, OK, I'm getting up. How I wish it could be the weekend for ever, especially now that Xavier is here. We had such a lovely time yesterday evening, singing along to CDs and making up the words when we weren't sure what they were. Apparently, in

French, that's called 'yogurt'. If you don't understand what you're hearing, you just invent the lyrics instead, or mumble nonsense and hope no one can tell. After we'd 'yogurted' our way through Amy's entire back catalogue (which is easy to do, as she's so slurry even I can't make out some of the words), we got out some of Mum and Dad's old records and did the same to them. We were laughing so hard, we were practically crying, giggling so much that my tummy muscles still hurt. (I even let out a little fart, but I don't think Xavier heard. God, I hope he didn't.) This is how 'You're The One That I Want' from *Grease* sounds to Xavier . . .

> *I've got shoes zair muzzer flying*
> *And the blues is to crawl*
> *Cos the flower you're zer flying*
> *It's elezzerfying*

I think I might like Xavier's version better.

During dinner, last night, Rosie texted to say she was a bit miffed that Xavier and I had left the market so early. I probably shouldn't have mentioned, in my reply, that we went to see Amy Winehouse's place. Stupid, I know, but I couldn't help it; I'm so used to telling Rosie everything. She said Manon was a huge Amy Winehouse fan, and that she would have loved the chance to come too. We can go again, I said, it's only up the road. Rosie texted back something along the lines of that if I wanted to get on with Manon, then I should make more of an effort. I didn't bother replying to that bit.

I'm sure Rosie will understand, when I explain how good it was for me to spend some time with Xavier on my own. We're getting closer, becoming good friends; I can feel it. I don't dare to hope that there's more to it, but maybe, just maybe . . . He didn't have to hang out with just me, all afternoon and evening, did he? I offered to call Rosie and Sky to see if they wanted to come and join us after dinner and he said, 'No, eez OK, just you and me.' He didn't have to give me a hug before he went to bed, but he chose to. And he didn't have to compliment me, either. He said, 'I like your hairs,' which made me blush and laugh at the same time. I didn't want to spoil the moment by correcting his English.

'Are you ready, Vix? We need to get a move on.'

I can hear Dad shouting from downstairs. No, I'm not ready, and I haven't had breakfast yet, but I can go without for once. Dad is giving Xavier a lift to the boys' school, on his way to work, and I'm coming along for the ride. It means I can't walk to school with Rosie, like I usually do, but it wouldn't be the same, anyway, with Manon trotting along beside us, all haughty and cold.

Dad says Xavier should sit in the front seat of the car, next to him, but he declines the offer and joins me in the back instead. He says it's because it would be weird to sit where the driver sits in France. I prefer to think that he just wants to sit next to me. Dad doesn't like it. 'I feel like a bleedin' taxi driver,' he says. But he catches my eye in the rear-view mirror, while he's driving, and gives me a little wink and a smile. He clearly likes Xavier and I think he also likes the fact that we're getting on so well. I pretend not to notice: it's embarrassing. Thankfully, he's stopped trying to impress Xavier with his prehistoric French. He chats away to him in English instead, about football and rugby – the universal men's languages. Luckily, I know a fair bit about both, so I can join in the conversation.

We're just parking up outside the boys' school, when Xavier spots two of the other French exchange boys walking along together. He winds down the car window and shouts something to them in French, which I guess must mean 'Hey come over here!' because they turn and walk towards the car. It's fairly obvious that they're trying to get a good look at me through the window, and it makes me feel very self-conscious. As they approach, Xavier grabs his backpack and opens the door, putting one foot on to the pavement. 'Sank you, Sir,' he says to Dad. And then, just as I think he's about to go without saying goodbye, he does something totally unexpected: he turns back to me and plants three big kisses on my cheeks, left, right and left again. In full view of his friends.

'*Ad t'aleur*, Veecks. See you later,' he says, putting his hand on my knee for a second, as he jumps out.

I will Dad to put his foot on the accelerator and go from nought to sixty in less than five seconds, so that Xavier and his friends, who are standing by the car, can't see how flustered I am. I know French people kiss each other all the time – Xavier's kissing his mates hello right now – but three kisses! And a knee touch too! It must mean . . . something. Of course, Dad doesn't speed off. He gently puts on the hand brake and suggests that I get out of the car too and come to join him in the front.

I don't move until Xavier and his friends have turned their backs and walked away. Then, smoothing down my skirt, I take a deep, calming breath, climb out and walk around to the front of the car.

'It's lovely to see you looking so happy,' says Dad, as I do up my seat belt. That's Dad code for, '*Ah, so you like the French boy, don't you?*'

'I'm fine, Dad,' I say. Which is Daughter code for, '*It's none of your business.*'

'Good. It's wonderful to see you looking so relaxed. I don't think I've heard you laugh that much for ages. Having Xavier here is obviously doing you the world of good. And,' he says, putting the car into first gear, 'I think it's probably good for all of us.'

'What do you mean?'

'I mean that as a family we've got into a bit of a depressing routine, dealing with your Mum's illness. I work too much, you do far too much to help around the house and Mum is miserable because she can do less and less. It's not your fault – and it's certainly not your Mum's – but I don't think it's been great for anyone.'

I nod. 'I guess.'

'You're fourteen – you should be out there having fun, not worrying about your mother. Xavier coming . . . it's . . . Well, having a stranger to stay makes everything a little more normal. Bizarrely.'

'I hadn't thought of it like that.'

'I don't suppose you had.' There's a tease in his voice. 'But then you've been too busy gazing at Xavier's dimples.'

I sink into the upholstery. 'Daaad! That's just so not true.'

'Come on, Vix. I might be old but I remember what it was like to be your age and to fancy someone. All those hormones . . . I reckon it's about time you got yourself a boyfriend.'

'God, you are so embarrassing. And patronising. If this is what it's going to be like every time I speak to a boy, I think I might just have to become a nun now.'

'We're not Catholic.'

'Well then, I'll just have to convert first. And then become a nun.'

'That would be a great shame, Vix. Not to mention that the shock would probably kill your fundamentally atheist grandma. I'm serious; I don't know about your mum but, as far as I'm concerned, if you and Xavier want to – how shall I put it – go out together, I won't stand in your way.'

'Thanks, Dad,' I say, unable to look him in the eye. I think I'll still be cringing at lunchtime. 'But it's not like that. I haven't even thought about Xavier in that way. Nothing's going to happen.'

Dad smiles. 'Sure you haven't. And the Pope's a Jehovah's Witness.'

Chapter 10
A Boy's Perspective

I'm still smiling about my conversation with Dad as I walk into my classroom. He's all right, my dad, even if he does sometimes say things that make me squirm. It's good to know that he likes Xavier and that he wouldn't mind if something happened between us. Not that it's going to . . . I can still feel the imprint of Xavier's kisses on my cheeks. I wonder what he said about me to his friends. I wonder what they said to him. Nothing, probably. Do I look OK today? Stupid question – I'm wearing my school 'uniform' of skinny jeans and a grey sweatshirt (we don't have an actual school uniform), with my hair tied in a ponytail and no make-up. It's what I always wear but, somehow, today, it feels very plain and boring. Maybe I'm finally growing out of the tomboy stage. Rosie and Sky are always saying I should make more of myself. Still, Xavier said he likes my 'hairs' . . .

I can't sit next to Rosie because everyone who has a French exchange student has to 'look after' them in joint lessons, so Manon has my usual place. Instead, I end up at a desk at the front of the classroom, next to Katy Owen, whose French exchange went down with glandular fever last week and had to cancel her entire stay. Poor Katy. She looks really miserable. Mind you, so do some of the other girls in my class, who clearly aren't getting on with their French exchanges. Imagine having to look after someone you can't stand, day and night, for four whole weeks. I am so lucky.

As we file out for breaktime, Lucy Reed stops me. She's wearing a big, fake grin. I know what's coming.

'Hey, Vix,' she purrs. 'So how's your French boy, then?'

I don't know what to say. Part of me likes the attention but, at the same time, I don't like it. What I like is being interesting for once in my life, and not just part of the classroom furniture. I'm the sort of girl who everybody gets on with – friendly, clever enough but not too clever, or too good at sport. I've never been bullied, or left out, or picked last, or anything like that. But nobody – apart from my friends – has ever been all that bothered about me, certainly not the loud, supposedly cool girls, like Lucy. I suppose I've never done anything to merit being interesting. On the other hand, her prurience makes me uncomfortable. The way I feel about Xavier is personal, something I'm still trying to work out in my head. If I'm honest, I'm not totally clear how I feel about him. I'm certainly not sure how he feels about me. And Lucy is the last person I want to discuss this with.

'He's nice,' I say, making it sound like I have no opinion one way or the other.

Lucy snorts. 'I got a good look at him at the station the other day. "Nice" isn't exactly the word I'd use to describe him. More like super fit. Don't tell me you haven't noticed!'

'It's none of your business,' I tell her. It's the stupidest thing I could say. It shows her she's getting to me and makes it look as if I have something to hide.

'Ooh la la! Touchy. So you have noticed!'

I sigh. 'Yes, he's fit. He's also a really great person. We had a fun weekend together. What else do you want me to say?'

'Sorry, sorry,' she says, putting her hand on my shoulder, as if we're mates. 'I wasn't having a go. I'm just interested, that's all.' She smiles. I think she must be angling for an introduction. I'm not going to offer one.

'No problem, Lucy. So how's your French exchange?'

She looks over her shoulder. Her exchange student, a small, mousy-looking girl, is standing in the corridor, waiting patiently for her.

'She's OK, a bit dull. I barely understand a single word she says.'

I shrug. 'Bummer. Listen, it's lovely chatting and all, but I really need to catch Rosie before breaktime ends.'

She won't give up. 'Sure . . . So I guess the party is at yours, then? And maybe you can get your guy to bring some of the other French boys. If you don't want to share him . . .'

I laugh. 'I don't think so, Lucy.' I really don't. I've never had a party at home and I'm not planning on starting now. Imagine Mum's face if half my year (and half of Facebook) turned up at my house, where everything has to be tidy and in its place, so she doesn't trip. Sick mums and house parties don't go together too well. Especially as I'd be the one clearing it all up afterwards.

'Well, if you change your mind, or feel like a night out sometime, let me know. We can all hang out. I can bring supplies.'

By supplies, she means alcohol. She's actually trying

to bribe me with alcohol! I can't be bothered to tell her that it wouldn't impress Xavier. He's already told me that he's been having a small glass of wine at dinner with his family ever since he was eleven. He can't see the point of drinking to get drunk, like some English teenagers do. Alcohol's not a big deal to him.

'OK, I'll let you know.'

'Cool,' she says. 'Do.'

Rosie is waiting for me outside. Alone, thankfully. She says Manon has gone to the loo, so we'll only have a couple of minutes to chat.

I give my best friend a hug. 'I miss not sitting next to you in class.'

'Yeah, me too. But it's only for a few weeks, and Manon's cool. It's not like we don't see each other all the time.'

'Yes, true. Listen, while she isn't here, there's something I want to talk to you about.'

'Go on . . .'

'It's Xavier.' I've been dying to tell her how my feelings have been developing, how I think I'm genuinely falling for him in a big way and how I suspect, just a tiny bit, even if I don't dare to admit it, that he might like me in return. What with Xavier staying at my house, and Manon at hers, we haven't had much time for our usual late-night messaging chats. I need to ask her advice on my next move. She's much more experienced in these things than me. 'I know we've all been joking about how gorgeous he is, and you and Sky have been teasing me, but I think I really like him. I mean LIKE him. In a "something could happen" way.'

Her reaction takes me by surprise. She stiffens. 'I'd keep your distance, Vix. Keep him as a friend. You don't want to get hurt, do you?'

'Why? What do you mean?'

'I mean, he's only here for a month and if you fall for him you'll get your heart broken. It's not worth it.'

'You've changed your tune. You told me to go for it. You were egging me on.'

'Yeah, well, I've been thinking about it and I just don't think it's a good idea to start up something with someone you probably won't ever see again.'

This isn't like Rosie at all. Usually, she's so encouraging, especially when she thinks I might be interested in someone. She's been telling me for years how much she'd like me to have a boyfriend. Just last week she was saying how great it would be if we could go out on double dates.

'Oh . . . I . . . I thought you'd be happy for me.'

'I wouldn't be much of a friend if I just stood by and watched you get hurt, would I?'

'No, I guess, but . . .' Manon is coming back. This isn't something I want to talk about in front of her. 'Anyway.'

Rosie squeezes my shoulder. 'We'll talk about it more another time, OK?'

'OK.'

I've got a very strong feeling that there must be more to this, something that she isn't telling me. But what?

It gnaws at me all afternoon but I have no opportunity to talk to her alone again. At lunch, we're joined by Manon and some of her French friends. Manon is as frosty with me as ever. She does say hello and she gives me two grudging air kisses, but she barely speaks to me after that. I understand that she'd rather catch up with her friends from home, in her own language, but still. It's ignorant.

I think I'm going to stop making an effort soon. I've tried complimenting her on her clothes, asked her what she likes doing at the weekends in Nice and attempted to find out about her family. All my questions are met with monosyllabic answers and a dismissive, patronising smile. Now, I'm running out of ways to begin a conversation with her. It's too much like hard work. I suppose I'm just going to have to accept that, for whatever reason, she doesn't like me. Well, guess what, *Mademoiselle* Up Yourself, the feeling is mutual. If only Rosie didn't seem to like her so much. They keep giggling together, like old friends, and I've noticed that Manon is wearing one of Rosie's favourite bracelets today. One that she was even loathe to lend Sky, when she asked, a few weeks ago.

I go straight home from school, even though Xavier won't be there. He's spending the evening with some of the other French boys and one of the parents is going to drop him back later. Dad won't be there either – he's got a work dinner – so I'm cooking spaghetti bolognese for Mum. I wish I hadn't promised her that now. I've got tons of coursework to do (which I didn't get around to at the weekend) and I don't feel very hungry. There's too much on my mind. I'll give myself a tiny portion and hope Mum doesn't notice.

She doesn't. Or if she does, she doesn't mention it. After dinner, I wash up as quickly as I can, then excuse myself and come up to my bedroom. I try to work, I really do, but after half an hour sitting staring at my textbooks, getting nowhere, I give up and go on to Facebook instead.

I need to talk to a good friend about everything. Ideally, I would chat to Sky, but she's staying with her half-sister Katie tonight and I don't want to interrupt their time together. They haven't known each other for long, but Sky's been so much happier and so much more confident since they met. She's stopped worrying about her stupid nose and she's got no time for the immature, rubbish boys, like Rich, who make her feel bad about herself. She's even got a new hobby, DJing, and she's getting pretty good at it.

Sometimes, I like to imagine that I've got a long-lost sister out there somewhere too. I know there's no way in a million years that my super straight dad has fathered a daughter he doesn't know about, but humour me. My sister wouldn't be Camden cool like Katie. No. My sister – let's call her Rachel (no reason, I just like the name) – would live on a farm in the countryside, far, far away, with acres and acres of private land, where I could learn to drive her car. She'd have quad bikes too and there'd be a lake where I could swim. And ponies. And dogs – great big, fluffy English sheepdogs. My friends could come to stay at weekends and we'd have picnics and camp out in the fields. Best of all, my sister would be terribly wise, with a long history of relationships. We'd sit by her enormous, roaring fire, with mugs of hot chocolate and toasted marshmallows (and perhaps, croissants), and I'd tell her all about Xavier and Rosie and Manon. She'd be able to tell me exactly what to do.

Unfortunately, my imaginary sister doesn't exist, which makes her worse than useless when it comes to giving advice. So, I do something I've never done before: I message Max to ask his opinion on my personal life.

Sometimes, I think, it's good to get advice from a friend who's not too close, for a more objective viewpoint. And, sometimes, it's useful to hear what a boy has to say. Especially if you're asking for advice about a boy. Max and I have been good friends since the summer, when he came to stay at his brother's house on my street. People say that if he hadn't gone out with Rosie (which was a whole big mess, as she didn't really fancy him), something might have happened between us. I don't know if that's true. Whatever might have been, he went back to boarding school and he has a new girlfriend. I'm happy being just mates and so is he.

We catch up a little, on what he's been doing at his wacky school, where the pupils make the rules and you can choose whether or not to go to lessons (weirdly, most people do). He asks how Rosie and Sky are, and tells me his rock star brother Rufus will be home from tour in a few weeks, so I should pop round to see him. When he asks how I am, I skirt around the issue for a while because I'm not sure where to start. If we were talking on the phone or face to face, I'd probably chicken out. In the end, I just go for it:

Me: *Can I ask you something? It's personal.*

Max: *Sure . . . Go ahead.*

Me: *OK, I've met this guy. Well, he's actually staying in my house. You know, the French exchange student I* told you about. I kind of like him. And I think he might like me too, but I'm not sure.

Max: *Yeah? Cool. So tell me more.*

I tell Max all about Xavier and the time we've spent together since he arrived, the way he acts around me, and the things he's said and done.

Max: *Vix, I think he definitely likes you.*

Me: *Really?*

Max: *Yes. Don't be so surprised. Why wouldn't he? You're cool and pretty and fun. A guy who wasn't in to you wouldn't want to spend so much time with you.*

Me: *But how can I be sure?*

Max: *Take it from me. I'm a guy, I know. So go for it!*

Me: *OK . . . thanks. There's something else. Rosie is being dead weird about it. She told me not to do anything about my feelings because I'm going to get my heart broken.*

Max: *Maybe she's jealous.*

Me: *No, I don't think so. She's got Laurie and she seems happy with him. I don't think she fancies Xavier at all.*

Max: *Well, maybe she doesn't want you to have a boyfriend. Maybe she likes you being single so you're always there for her.*

Me: *No, it's not that either. I'm sure.*

Max: *Just ignore her then. It's your life. Like I said, I* *think you should go for it. Your heart might get broken, but maybe it won't. But if you don't do anything you'll never know, will you? You've got to take risks sometimes if you want anything good to happen.*

Me: *I know you're right. It's not that I'm scared. But I don't know where to start.*

I don't want to tell him I've never had a boyfriend, even though he's probably guessed.

How do I let Xavier know that I like him and want something to happen? What do I do? What do I say?

Max: *There aren't any rules. Just be yourself, Vix. If he likes you back, and I'm sure he does, it will happen naturally.*

I wrap up the conversation after that because I'm not sure what else to say, and Xavier will be back soon, and if I don't do some homework I will get into serious trouble at school tomorrow. But I can't stop thinking about what Max said. Be myself? That's easy. But it doesn't help at all. I've always been myself and nothing has ever happened 'naturally' before, not with anyone. Maybe 'being myself' is the problem. Maybe I'm destined to be single for ever.

Chapter 11
My Fairy Godmother

When I first started helping to look after Mum, I used to think of myself as a sort of Cinderella (without the Ugly Sisters or the rags). If I was doing a chore I really hated – cleaning the bathroom, say – I'd shut my eyes as tightly as I could and will a Fairy Godmother to appear. With a wave of her magic wand, she'd not only make all the cleaning products disappear, she'd also make Mum better – and not just until midnight. Then she'd whisk me off in a Formula One racing car (horses and carriages are far too clunky) to a fabulous theme park, where all my friends would be waiting. At the time, I was far too young to appreciate boys, so there was never a

Prince Charming figure in my fantasy. But if there had been, I'm sure he'd have been a lot like Xavier. So maybe all those years of wishing did work after all . . .

'Veecks?' A sleepy-looking Xavier jolts me out of my daydreams. I was hoping to have finished cleaning the bathroom before he emerged from his bedroom. I don't want him to know that when's Dad's away I get up a full half-hour before him every day, or that this morning I've already helped Mum out of bed, got her dressed, taken her downstairs and made her coffee. He rubs his eyes. 'Vot are you doing?'

It must be fairly obvious. I have a cloth in one hand and a can of Mr Muscle in the other. I resist the temptation to say something sarcastic like 'I'm baking a cake' because I've learned that sarcasm doesn't translate very well, and that, by the time I've explained that I'm joking, it won't seem remotely clever or funny any more. 'I'm cleaning.'

'Yes, but why? Why before school?'

'Because the bath is dirty. And because Mum asked me to. I was supposed to do it last night but didn't have time. It's no big deal.'

'Ah, OK. Your muzzer, she eez OK? She does not work, no?'

I guess he's wondering why she can't clean the bathroom herself.

'No, she doesn't work at the moment . . .' I leave the statement hanging. Mum used to be a teacher. She was medically retired a few years ago. She'll never be able to go back, but Xavier doesn't need to know that.

'She eez sick?'

It's the question I've been dreading. I take a deep breath. I could still change my mind and tell him the truth. And maybe I would, if he didn't look so concerned and sympathetic. The last thing I want from him is his pity.

'She hurt her legs. Um, in an accident. It just means she can't walk properly or do stuff around the house for a while.' I smile. 'I really don't mind helping out.'

I'm not sure if he believes me – although I suppose there's no reason why he shouldn't – but, thankfully, he doesn't ask for any more details. 'She will get bettair soon,' he says, in a comforting tone. He puts his hand on my shoulder and I tingle, all the way down to my fingertips.

'Sure she will.'

'So I 'elp you now?'

I look at him, incredulous. 'Seriously?'

'Why not? I can clean also.'

'No, you're a guest. It wouldn't be right. Anyway, you need to get ready for school.'

'*Bof.* Wiz two eet eez quickair.'

'OK, then. That would be great. Thanks.' Before he can change his mind, I find him another cloth and hand him the can of cleaning fluid, pointing him in the direction of the sink. He sets to work, humming some of the *Grease* yogurt lyrics we made up as he goes along. 'Ya da wada wada, you da wada wada, ooh ooh oh.'

I join in on the 'ooh ooh oohs' and we both giggle. Max should be proud of me. I am totally 'being myself' – I can't think of any activity less glamorous or pretentious than cleaning. And cleaning with Xavier is (almost) fun. Come to think of it, doing pretty much anything with Xavier would be fun or, certainly, more bearable. I should ask him if he'll come to the dentist with me and help me with my maths coursework.

'Zair,' he says, when he's finished. His effort has been a bit slapdash and he's forgotten to wipe around the taps, but who cares? 'All fineeshed.'

I smile at him in the (slightly smeary) bathroom cabinet mirror and he grins back at me. Funny how things turn out. I'd always imagined my Fairy Godmother to be a slightly plump, middle-aged woman with a perm, a pink tutu and a magic wand, not a fit French boy with wavy hair, dark-wash jeans and a can of Mr Muscle. Perhaps Xavier is my Prince Charming and Fairy Godmother rolled into one. Although he can't make Mum better. Nobody can do that, not even the brain scientists.

I leave him to take a shower while I go into my bedroom to finish getting ready for school. We meet downstairs, in the kitchen. Mum is at the table, where I left her, looking at her laptop. She makes small talk with us while we eat our cereal, and then, before I can stop him, Xavier comes out with, 'I am very sorry to 'ear of your accidont, *Madame*.'

Whoops! When I told him my little white lie, I didn't expect him to say anything to Mum. That was stupid of me. I should have warned him not to mention it, said that she was touchy about it. I don't want Mum to think I'm ashamed of her illness.

Mum raises her eyebrows at me. Her expression reads, 'We'll discuss this later.'

I glance back at her, innocently, and will her not to correct Xavier.

'Thank you, Xavier,' she says. 'That's very kind of you. Actually, while you're both here, I wanted to ask you something. My friend Jane has just emailed. She's got a spare ticket for the theatre tonight and wonders if I'd like to go with her. She said she could pick me up at six and take me for a bite to eat first. Would you mind if I wasn't here tonight? Could you manage on your own? It'll only be for a few hours.'

I try not to look too happy. Do I mind having to

spend the evening alone with Xavier? Hardly. Do I mind having the house to ourselves for a few hours? Hell no!

'Sure, Mum, that's fine with me. It'll be so good for you to get out. Um, that's if it's OK with you, Xavier?'

He looks puzzled. Perhaps Mum was talking too fast. Sometimes I forget that his English isn't perfect and he can't always keep up.

'My mum is going out tonight, so we'll have to stay alone here. Is that OK?'

He grins. '*Mais oui*, of course. Perhaps I can cook something *Français*, as I promised?'

'Cool,' I say. 'That would be perfect. There you go, Mum. All sorted. Go out and have a good time. We'll be fine.'

Mum is hesitant. 'Perhaps I should clear it with the school. I'm not sure if I'm allowed to leave Xavier unsupervised.'

'Oh, no, I wouldn't bother with that. Like you said, it's only for a few hours. And you know we're both very responsible. Well, you know I am, anyway.'

She nods. 'OK, then.' Although neither of us dares to say it, we're both aware that, these days, I'm usually the one who looks after her, and not the other way around.

I smile. 'I promise we won't have any wild parties or set fire to the kitchen.'

Today, with no Dad around to give us a lift, we're

meeting Rosie and Manon at the end of the street, so that we can all walk to school together. (Xavier now feels confident enough in Camden to make the last part of the journey on his own.) It's the first time Rosie has seen me with him since our little chat, a couple of days ago, and I feel very self-conscious. As we head towards her, I know she's watching how I act with him, reading my body language and trying to work out what's going on between us. I'm giving nothing away; I don't want another lecture. I try to behave as coolly as I can, walking fast and looking straight ahead until I'm close enough to make eye contact with her. Then I smile my broadest smile, greet her and Manon, and start chatting about the test we've got today. I even let Manon monopolise Xavier all the way to school, pretending that it doesn't bother me.

Xavier leaves us at the school gates.

'See you laytair, Veecks,' he says, as he kisses me goodbye (he kisses the others too). I maintain my composure, giving him a shy smile only when I'm sure the others can't see.

He's just begun to walk away when Rosie calls him back. 'I forgot to say, do you want to come out for coffee with us after school? I've said I'd take Manon and a couple of her friends to Tupelo Honey. You should both come too. And I'm going to text Sky to see if she fancies it.'

I don't know what to say. I try to catch Xavier's eye to see his reaction but he just grins at me, enigmatically. Maybe he doesn't understand. After what Rosie said the other day, I certainly don't want to make a big thing about having time alone with Xavier tonight, or to tell her that he's cooking for me. Never mind, I suppose we can always have coffee with the others and then go home and have dinner later.

I'm just about to say, 'OK, that would be nice,' when Xavier answers instead.

'We cannot come tonight, sorry,' he says, with the type of assurance that nobody would dare to question. 'I promise to make dinair for Veecks's muzzair. Anuzzer night, per'aps.'

So he's fibbed! And I didn't even ask him to. Either he doesn't want to go out with the others or he really does want to spend time alone with me. God, I hope it's the latter. I seriously cannot wait until tonight.

Chapter 12
The Day After

Rosie comes to find me at breaktime. I'm really glad to see that she's on her own for once, without Manon, because I am absolutely dying to tell her about everything that happened after Mum went out last night. I need to get it off my chest and I could do with her perspective. By the time I got to bed it was too late to text her or Sky. And there was no time before school this morning. Not being able to talk about it is driving me a little bit bonkers.

But she doesn't seem to notice that I'm bursting to spill. Before I can begin, she says, 'We really need to talk, Vix,' and she sounds ominously serious. That throws me.

Today, of all days, I am not in the mood for serious. 'Can we have lunch together today?' she asks. 'Just you and me?'

I nod, vigorously. 'I'd like that.' She has no idea how much. 'And, actually, I need to speak to you as well. I've got *loads* of stuff to tell you . . .'

I leave the sentence hanging in the air, enticingly, hoping that she'll ask me what it is that I want to talk about now, and let me start telling her, because I'm not sure I can keep it all inside until lunchtime. But she doesn't. She just puts her hand on my shoulder, gives it a little squeeze, and says, 'OK, cool, see you later, then,' and announces that she has to go to the loo before her next class.

And then she's gone, and I'm still standing in the same spot, looking like a demented fish, with my mouth hanging open. I've got no idea what she wants to talk to me about. Whatever it is can't be as important as what I need to say. Maybe she feels bad about Manon being mean to me and is trying to make things right again. That would be good. I miss Rosie. It feels like ages since I've spent proper time with her, even if it is only about a week.

Somehow, I make it through the morning's classes without getting into trouble for daydreaming or doodling. I meet Rosie at the entrance to the school canteen and, even though I've got no appetite at all (despite not eating any breakfast), we grab some ready-made sandwiches and yogurts, so we can take them outside to our favourite lunch spot, a quiet area just behind the science block, where hardly anybody comes. We sit down on a step and open our sandwiches and Rosie starts eating hers, while I play about with mine. I'm still dying to talk but I've had too much time to think about everything and now my thoughts are all jumbled up, and I don't know where to begin. Maybe I'll let her go first, after all.

'So . . .' I say, grinning at Rosie.

'So . . .' She grins back.

'You wanted to talk to me about something?'

'I did. That's right. Didn't you want to tell me something too?'

'Yes . . . but you go first.'

'OK . . .' She seems reticent, like she's having second thoughts. 'It's, er, about Manon.'

'Aha. I thought so.' Reassured, I take a bite of my sandwich.

'Look, it seems like you're not exactly getting on, and it's a bit awkward for me, what with her staying with me and you being my best friend and everything.'

'I know. I'm sorry. It's not like I haven't tried. It's weird for me too.'

She smiles. 'It's just . . . you could make it a lot easier.'

Irritated, I put my sandwich back in the packet and place it on the step. 'How do you mean I could make it easier? She's the one who didn't like me from the start. I didn't do or say anything bad to her.'

'I know. It's not that. Of course you didn't. It's more about . . . Xavier.'

'Xavier? What about him?' I'm aware I sound defensive. I can't help it.

'Manon *really* likes Xavier. You must have noticed – she's not exactly subtle about it.'

I snort. 'Yeah, that's for sure.'

'She thinks you've got in the way.'

It all makes perfect sense now. 'So that's why she doesn't like me! She's jealous! I couldn't work out what I'd done.'

'She doesn't not like you. She thinks you're all right, actually. But she's miffed that you've come between her and Xavier. It's also obvious to her that you like him and that you're after him.'

'It's not exactly like that!'

'Vix, there's something you need to know. She told me that they've got something going on, back in France.'

My stomach lurches horribly, the piece of sandwich I've just swallowed sticking halfway down my throat.

'What do you mean?' I try not to sound panicky. 'He says he hardly knows her. They go to the same school, that's all.'

'Well, that's not what she told me. She said that they'd flirted at a party and that they were getting quite close before the exchange. All her friends said something was definitely going to happen between them in London. And then she got here and Xavier met you, and everything changed.'

'Oh! Is that all? They flirted at a party – which she could have imagined – and her friends said something might happen – which they probably only said because it was what she wanted to hear.' I'm so relieved, I'm practically laughing. 'Sorry, Rosie, but I think it's all in her head. Do you know what? Between you and I, I don't even think Xavier likes her that much as a friend. He never looks that happy when she talks to him and he doesn't seem to want to spend any time with her. He never, ever mentions her or says he wants to hang out with her.'

She doesn't look at me. 'Maybe that's because you're always there.'

'So what? If he really liked her, not just in her fantasies, that wouldn't matter.'

Rosie looks uncomfortable. 'I'm not getting at you, Vix. Please don't get so upset about this. She just thinks you've got in the way, distracted him.'

But I am upset. 'Distracted him? Doesn't he have a mind of his own? And anyway, even if it were all my fault, which is ridiculous, how was I supposed to know that she thought she had something going on with him?'

'You weren't. But you do now.'

'So what am I supposed to do? It's not like I can help it if he likes me.'

'You could step aside. You could act like you're not interested until he gets the message and gives up. I'm just asking you nicely to please back off. Then we can all be friends and it will all be so much easier.'

'It's not that simple,' I say quietly. 'I like him. A lot.'

'I know you think you do, hon,' says Rosie. I roll my eyes. I realise she means to be sweet, but it just comes across as patronising. 'But you hardly know him. Do you really think you'd like him that much, if he weren't French? Maybe it's just the cute accent and the fact he dresses differently from the guys we know. If you put him in a hoodie and trainers, cut his hair differently and made him talk with a London accent, you probably wouldn't look at him twice.'

I've tried to keep calm but I'm angry now. 'That's total crap, Rosie. I've spent loads of time with him, talking about all sorts of stuff. I know I really do like him. And why the hell should I care about Manon's feelings, when I don't even know her? She's not my friend. She's just some girl who you've only known for a few days! It's not as if you or Sky had feelings for someone first – that would be different. I don't owe Manon anything. Anyway, I can't tell Xavier who he should fancy. If he prefers me, that's not my fault. That's just life. Or, *c'est la vie*, as Manon would probably say.'

'God, Vix, calm down. I don't want to fall out over this. I was just trying to have a friendly chat. What's happened to you? You're not yourself at all today.'

She's right, I'm not acting like 'myself' today, and do you know what? I feel bloody brilliant about it. I wouldn't normally be this confident or assertive. Usually, I would back down, apologise even though I haven't done anything wrong, and contemplate walking away so that Manon could continue to develop her relationship with Xavier, imaginary or not. Anything for an easy life, anything to make other people happy.

But that was the old me, the me that had no experience, the me who thought I wasn't good enough or pretty enough, the me who always put other people first. That was the me who had never been kissed, the me who had nothing to lose because I'd never won anything.

That me doesn't exist any more. This is the new, improved me. For, what nobody knows yet – that thing that I've been bursting to talk about – is that last night, after school, something did happen between Xavier and me.

I shrug. 'I don't want to fall out with you either, Rosie. But what you're asking isn't fair. We've been friends for ever. It feels like you're putting Manon's feelings before mine. That hurts.'

'I'm sorry,' says Rosie, and I can tell she means it. 'It's not what I intended to do. I just want everyone to get on. I had no idea you felt so strongly about this. You're right. It isn't fair.' She gives me a brave little smile. 'So, let's change the subject. What was it you were going to tell me?'

I take a deep breath, open my mouth, and then shut it again. I should tell her. I planned to tell her. A big part of me still wants to tell her. God, I always imagined she'd be the first person I'd tell about something this momentous. But how can I tell her now?

'Nothing,' I say, turning away to stare pointlessly at the uniform grey bricks of the science block. 'It's not important.'

Chapter 13

About Last Night

I decide to tell Sky instead. She is equally my best friend, although I haven't known her for quite as long and she doesn't go to my school. There are actually some things it's easier to talk to her about than Rosie – like my worries about Mum – because she hasn't always had a straightforward time with her parents, either.

'So go on then, spill,' she says excitedly, once I've told her why I'm there. I've popped round after school on the pretext of borrowing a book. The truth is, I would have spontaneously combusted if I hadn't confided in someone.

'I'm not really sure where to start . . .' I can't stop

smiling. It feels like somebody has attached puppet hooks to my jaw and is pulling them upwards. My lips are starting to ache.

'How about at the beginning? When you got home from school with Xavier.'

'OK. So, we came in and Xavier looked at me in this really sweet, meaningful way and said he was going to go to Sainsbury's and buy some food for dinner, and then he asked me if there was anything I don't like to eat and where the shopping bags were . . .'

Sky giggles. 'I want all the facts, hon,' she says, 'but maybe not in that much detail. Skip to the interesting part!'

'OK, sorry. I was just remembering how it all happened in my head. It's kind of hard to edit. OK. So, he went to Sainsbury's and bought some food for dinner. And we ate it. And then we sort of kissed.'

Sky rolls her eyes at me. 'Vix, you can give me a bit more detail than that! What did he make? Something really romantic and French?'

'I don't know what it was. It was kind of weird, actually. Not at all what I was expecting. It was this dish made of macaroni with fried eggs and olive oil.'

'Yeah, sounds weird . . . I guess that could be OK . . .'

'It was really tasty, believe it or not, although I'd probably have pretended I liked it even if I didn't, so as not to be rude. Xavier says it's his favourite food at home, sort of comfort food. His mum used to make it for him when he was a kid and she showed him how to do it. And then we had crème caramels – although he didn't make those, he just bought them.'

'Yum. So how did you end up . . . you know . . .'

'Well . . .'

It's a good question. How did it happen? I'm still not entirely sure. Right up to the moment that it did happen, I still wasn't certain that it was going to, or that Xavier properly liked me. He was shyer than usual all evening, more jokey, even putting me down a bit. But at the same time, I kept catching him looking at me, when he didn't think I could tell, and when we were in the kitchen he brushed against my leg and my elbow more times than could have been accidental. Looking back, I guess he must have been nervous.

'To tell the truth, in the end, I sort of kissed him,' I admit, blushing at the memory. I screw up my face, like it's a bit painful to think about.

'Seriously?'

'Yes. Is that bad? Should I not have?'

'God, no. There's nothing wrong with it at all. I'm just surprised.'

'Really? I couldn't help myself. We were doing this stupid kind of dance around each other all night, and I kept thinking something was going to happen, and then it didn't, and in the end I just did it — spontaneously, without thinking. We were on the sofa by then, in the living room, sitting dead close together with our legs touching, talking about rubbish, and I suddenly got the urge to kiss him. It just seemed like the obvious thing to do. If I'd thought about it too much I'd have chickened out. Luckily, he kissed me back!'

'Good for you, Vix!' She slaps me on the back, playfully.

'I don't think he could tell that I haven't . . .' I pause, remembering just in time that Sky doesn't know I've never kissed anybody before, making what I did even more extraordinary and brave. ' . . . that I don't have much experience.'

'Course he couldn't, hon. And I'm sure he wouldn't care, anyway. So was it good?'

'God, yeah.' I can't help smiling at the memory. 'It was amazing. Just perfect. He's got such lovely lips. I think I could have done it for ever. Except then Mum came home from the theatre with her friend and we had to jump apart and pretend we'd just been watching TV.'

'Did she believe you?'

'I don't know. I think so. She hasn't said anything, anyway.'

'Hmmm,' says Sky, unconvinced. 'I'm sure she wouldn't

have a problem with it, anyway.'

'I don't think so. I know Dad will definitely be pleased though, when I get to tell him we're going out.' I recount our conversation in the car. 'He told me something was going to happen and I said of course it wouldn't. I still can't quite believe it has.'

'Ah, I'm so happy for you, hon,' says Sky, giving me a little hug. 'You totally deserve it.'

'Thanks, Sky.' I look down at the carpet. 'I just wish everyone could be so happy for us. Rosie isn't going to be. I meant to tell her but I couldn't. She thinks the sun shines out of Manon's —'

'Vix! No she doesn't.'

'She so does. Apparently, Manon has a claim on Xavier just because she knew him first and fancies him.'

'Manon's OK, really. Look at it from her point of view. If you fancied a guy for ages and then he went off to France and met someone else, right in front of you, you'd be gutted too.'

'I guess. When you put it that way. But I've tried with her, Sky, and she's so hostile. If she'd been friendlier from the start, and I'd figured out how she felt about Xavier, maybe I wouldn't have done anything. Or at least I'd have known the score. What really gets me is that she's – all of this – is coming between me and Rosie, which is horrible.'

'You'll sort it out, hon, you always do,' says Sky, no doubt referring to the last time Rosie and I had a disagreement, over the way she treated Max.

'I know. But in the meantime . . .'

'You want me to tell her for you?'

I nod, solemnly.

'I'd rather you did it yourself, Vix. But I understand why you feel you can't. OK, consider it done. But promise me you'll talk to her soon.'

'I promise.'

She hugs me again. 'I am so super happy for you, Vix. I'm so glad you're finally getting to have some fun. Except, now I'm the only one without a boyfriend!'

Chapter 14

Cloud 5800957

Monday morning. It feels really awkward walking to school with Rosie today, even though we've done it virtually every morning since we were eleven. Now I wish I'd texted her and told her I'd see her there instead, but old habits die hard. Even though I've had no confirmation, I know Sky will now have told her that Xavier and I got together the other night, and I also know that she will be pissed off with me about that. Manon (who, of course, is with us) must know too. Worse, Rosie will be hurt and annoyed that I didn't feel able to tell her about it myself during our lunchtime chat. I do feel bad about that. It just seemed as if she was on Manon's side, not mine, and that stings.

We've barely spoken since then. I know I promised Sky that I'd talk to her, but it hasn't happened yet. It's not that we've fallen out, more like we've put our friendship on hold until Manon is back across the Channel and out of the picture. How can we sort things out when Manon goes everywhere that Rosie goes – home, school, even our favourite after-school cafés? Why can't she just hang around with some of her French friends for a change? Why doesn't Rosie ask her to?

On the plus side, not seeing Rosie meant that I got to spend almost the whole weekend alone with Xavier, which was amazing. On Saturday we went to the go-karting track, which I've been dying to do for ages but never managed because nobody else has ever wanted to go with me. Sky is too scared and doesn't like fast cars and Rosie thinks go-karting is boring (even though she's never tried it) and that the helmet will mess up her hair (she's right, but so what?). I was much better at it than Xavier, but I let him win a couple of times, because I didn't want to show him up (or show off).

We spent all of Saturday night and most of last night snogging in my room until really late. I had no idea that kissing could be so varied and so exciting and so much fun, or that it was possible to snog for hours without getting bored, or getting mouth cramp. It must be because Xavier is such a good kisser (I'm absolutely certain I'm right about this, even though I don't have anyone else to compare him with), and possibly because he's French. They invented it, didn't they? Snogging, I mean. Isn't that why it's called French kissing? Xavier says they don't call it French kissing in France – he thinks it's hilarious that we do. He and his friends call it 'tongue soup' which is a bit gross. Not surprisingly, I barely got any of my coursework done again this weekend. Never mind, I'm sure I can catch up soon. I overslept a little this morning, which meant that I didn't have time to do everything I was supposed to do for Mum. I've never done that before, and she said she didn't mind; but I think she did, really. I'll make it up to her when Xavier has gone back. Oh God, that is something I do not want to think about. I'm going to pretend that it will never happen.

We walk along, side by side, so close that we're almost, but not quite, touching. Occasionally, his elbow jostles against my forearm, or his fingertips brush against mine, and I feel little sparks of pleasure shooting out into my tummy. I want to grab his hand and hold it properly; but I'm too shy, and I'm not sure if he wants to do the same, or whether that will make Rosie and Manon even angrier. They're marching several paces ahead of us, pretending we're not there. Manon didn't even bother to greet me today; she simply nodded and rolled her eyes at me. Do you know what? I honestly don't care. At least I don't have to pretend I like her any more.

And now we're at the school gates and it's time to say goodbye. I wish Xavier could come in with me and spend the day in my classes; I'm not sure how I'm going to manage without him until four p.m. I'm aware that sounds pathetic. Isn't it weird how you can worry about missing someone you'd never even dreamed of meeting a few weeks ago?

'See you later, Xavier. Have a good day,' I say. I flash him a coy little smile. I expect him to wish me the same, to give me a quick peck on both cheeks, and then to turn and walk away.

But he doesn't. He says, 'Goodbye, Veecks.' And then he grabs my face in both his hands and kisses me. He kisses me properly, deeply, as if he really means it and wants everyone to know that we're together. The kiss takes me by surprise and, for a moment, I can't relax into it. I know that people are watching, not just Rosie and Manon but girls in my year too, girls like big mouth Lucy Reed, whose mum has just dropped her off outside the school gate. I close my eyes tight to shut them all out and let myself melt into the kiss. Soon, I don't care who can see us; I don't care about any of them. I don't care if the news is all around the school in a few hours. I only care about the kiss. For thirty gorgeous, exquisite seconds, nothing else matters, nothing at all: not the fact that Manon clearly now hates me so much that she'd probably like to chop my head off with a guillotine, French Revolution style; not the fact that Rosie is being weird with me; not even my Mum's illness. I'm as happy as happy can be. I'm floating high above the world, weightless and absolutely free. I'm on cloud . . . a cloud that's way, way higher than nine. I must be on at least cloud one hundred. No, one hundred thousand. Or even higher: somewhere in the millions . . . How about cloud five million, eight hundred thousand, nine hundred and fifty-seven? Yes, that's my personal happiness cloud. I don't ever want to come down from it.

Too soon, Xavier pulls away and the world roars back into focus. I had no idea so many people were standing around. It seems as if almost half the school has arrived in the last few seconds, and Xavier and I are the main attraction. Looking into the faces of the crowd, I feel like I've accidentally just auditioned for a new type of reality TV show: *Britain's Most Talented Kisser*. Somebody is clapping, someone else calling out, 'Get a room, guys!' and Lucy Reed is holding her mobile up in the air; I think she might actually be filming us. My cheeks are glowing hot and I'm not sure whether to feel proud of myself or deeply ashamed. Nothing like this has ever happened to me before.

I try to catch Rosie's eye; she looks shocked and disapproving. Manon has her arms folded, a look of disdain on her face. I'm sure I'm going to have to pay for what just happened. I'm also aware that cloud five million, eight hundred thousand, nine hundred and fifty-seven is very, very high up. That means there's a hell of a long way to fall.

Chapter 15

Sailing Away

My mum is getting worse, little by little. As much as she denies it, and as much as I try to pretend that it's not happening, the signs are obvious. Most days now, her walking is so unsteady that she can't even manage two steps without her stick. She's in so much pain that she's given in and started taking the strong painkillers she hates, and they're making her woozy and dizzy and sick. She can't sleep a wink at night, but she is so tired during the day that she usually falls asleep in the afternoons in her armchair, like an old lady.

She says she loved going to the theatre last week with her friend, only it did her in; she doesn't think she can attempt a trip out like that again for a long time. I think she might be feeling depressed. I don't blame her, anyone in her position would be. She's on her own almost all the time, stuck in the house, unable to concentrate on anything for long. She's bored and lonely and miserable.

I feel bad for her, I really do; but the problem is, I don't want to be the solution. I know it's selfish of me, but I don't want to spend all my spare time talking to Mum when I'm at home. It's already taking longer and longer to help her get dressed in the mornings and to get ready for bed in the evenings. Dad says he's going to try to rearrange his schedule so he can come home from work earlier and be around to help more, but it's not enough. I can't do everything myself in the meantime, especially when I'm trying to keep the amount I do from Xavier. Now, when Dad's not at home, I get up almost an hour earlier than Xavier and, at night, I pretend that I'm going to bed, then creep into Mum's room to help her. It's crazy, but I'm sneaking around behind Mum and Dad's backs to spend private time with Xavier, and sneaking around behind his back to help Mum get washed and dressed. No wonder I feel stressed out most of the time.

Today, I've come home from school, hoping to spend some time with Xavier, as well as everything else I need to do, and now Mum is telling me we hardly have any food in the house, so I need to go to Sainsbury's for her too. She was supposed to do an internet shop, but I have a suspicion that her hands have been playing up this week, making it hard to type on the keyboard. Or maybe she's just forgotten. Her memory has been a bit dodgy lately too, which is really scary.

'Can't we make do with whatever's in the cupboard tonight?' I ask.

She's not in the mood for a discussion. 'No. We need to eat properly and there's nothing fresh. I'd like you to get some chicken and vegetables, and we need milk and eggs too.' She points to her handbag. 'There's some cash in my purse. Please could you take it and go to Sainsbury's now.'

I turn away and make a face. 'OK. Come on, then, Xavier,' I say, taking the money from her bag and shoving the folded notes into my purse. I'm pretty sure he hasn't understood my conversation with Mum. We were going too fast for him. 'We need to go shopping, get some stuff in for dinner,' I explain. 'If you don't mind coming?'

'Ah, OK,' he says, getting up from the sofa. I hand him the coat he's just taken off. I don't say goodbye to Mum.

Xavier holds my hand as we walk along the street. 'You appear sad,' he says. 'Eez it your muzzer? You worry about her broken legs?'

'Something like that.' I smile at him. He's so sweet. For a moment I have second thoughts about not telling him the truth, then change my mind instantly. Even if I wanted to come clean about the fact that Mum hasn't had an accident but has a disease that's getting worse, I still couldn't do it. First, he'd be angry that I'd lied. Then he'd start asking questions and then I'd have to explain everything. How can you tell your new boyfriend that sometimes your mum doesn't make it to the loo in time? Both ends. That she has to wear pads, like a nappy? It's really embarrassing and gross and totally unromantic and, anyway, she'd hate it too if she thought I'd told anyone that.

So I don't tell him. Instead, I stop walking, turn my body around to face him, and kiss him hard on the mouth. I've discovered that kissing can be a great distraction. He kisses me back, just like I hope he will and soon I realise that I don't feel angry or upset about Mum any more.

When I open my eyes, I notice that we're standing by the steps that lead down to Regent's Canal. It's growing dark now, and I'm not supposed to walk along the canal at night (or even during the day, without an adult), but I want a few minutes' privacy with Xavier, and I figure I'll be safe if he's there. It feels naughty and exciting and a bit dangerous, which is exactly what I need right now. 'Come on,' I say, taking his hand. 'Let's go down here.'

He looks puzzled. 'Zee supermarket?'

'We'll go there in a bit. But you've never seen the canal, have you? Only the bit at Camden Lock. It runs for miles, all the way from Little Venice into the Thames, and you can walk along all the way, past the back of the zoo, through the park, the back of King's Cross. It's cool.'

'OK,' he says, letting me lead him.

We walk along the canal for a while, hand in hand. There's nobody dodgy around, just a few dog walkers and some cyclists heading home from work. I notice that the water looks cleaner and more inviting at night, with the lamps from the towpath reflected in it; you can't see the cans and food wrappers that people have thrown in.

'I'd like to live on a barge,' I say, as we pass somebody's colourful houseboat. 'Going up and down canals all day, being totally free. I'd love it. Wouldn't you?'

Xavier turns up his nose at my suggestion. 'Rather a yacht.' He grins. 'Like zee ones in zee port in Nice.'

I laugh, picturing Xavier as a millionaire playboy and me in a glamorous bikini, sipping ice-cold drinks on the deck. 'Yeah, a yacht would be cool too. I guess they go faster. And it's sunny and you can go way out to sea. Have you ever been on one?'

'*Non,*' he says. 'Only a pedalo.'

I laugh. 'Not quite the same.'

Xavier laughs too, then puts his hands around my waist and gently pushes me back towards the wall, so we're out of the way of anyone passing by. He kisses me and, even though it's chilly and dark and we're in the middle of Camden Town, I close my eyes and imagine we're on a yacht together, basking in the sun, without a care in the world. Sailing away from it all.

I don't know how long we kiss for, but something, a bicycle bell perhaps, drags me back into the real world and makes me stop and check my watch. 'We'd better get the shopping,' I say. 'Come on. We'll come back here another time and we'll walk along to the back of London Zoo. You can see some of the animals for free that way. Maybe at the weekend.'

We come up the stairs just by Sainsbury's, on the other side of the road. I ask Xavier to grab a basket and then we weave around the store as quickly as we can, grabbing the things Mum has asked for. I know where everything is so well that Xavier can barely keep up with me.

When we come into the house, Dad is home, much earlier than expected. At least, I think, with relief, I don't have to cook tonight too. 'Your mum wants to talk to you,' he says, raising an eyebrow. He gets up from the sofa. 'I'll leave you to it.' He takes the bag of groceries from my hands, and heads for the kitchen.

'Eef eet eez OK, I am going to take a shower before dinair,' says Xavier.

'Absolutely,' says Mum, in a tone that signifies she wants him out of the way so she can tell me off. She waits until he's disappeared up the stairs and then starts. 'Where on earth have you been? The shops are only five minutes away.

You've been gone for over an hour. I was starting to get worried.'

'Yeah, sorry, we kind of lost track of time. It took a while to find everything.'

'Don't give me that. I wasn't born yesterday. You've obviously been off somewhere with Xavier.'

I should just apologise and promise not to do it again, but the censorious tone of her voice is winding me up. 'So what if I have? I got the shopping too. Can't I have even a little bit of time to myself after school?'

'If you'd got the shopping first, and then asked, it would have been fine.'

'Would it? Because then you'd have told me it was time to do my homework, or cook for you, or whatever. You don't seem to want me to hang out with Xavier. Every time I'm alone with him you call me to do something.'

'That's not true. But, if I'm being honest, I don't really think you should be romantically involved with a boy who is staying in our house. I don't feel comfortable about it.'

I huff. 'Dad doesn't mind. He's even pleased about it. You're only saying that because you want all my time for yourself! You're jealous.'

'Don't be ridiculous, Victoria. I'm thinking about you. He's only here for a few weeks. I'm worried you're getting too serious and you're going to get hurt when he leaves.'

She's expressing my own fears and I don't want to hear

them. 'I don't believe you. The truth is, whatever you say, you've never wanted me to have a boyfriend, have you? It would suit you if I were single for the rest of my life, so I can look after you, wouldn't it?'

'Victoria, you know that's not true.'

'It's Vix, not Victoria!' I scream. 'You never listen to me. You don't even know who I am. Well, I'm sick of not having a life. You stop me seeing my friends, you don't want me to have a boyfriend and you expect me to be your slave too. It's not fair and I've had enough! If you don't think I'm good enough then go and find yourself another slave!'

Mum looks shocked and hurt and angry too. If she could get out of her chair without help I think she'd come right over and slap me. I stare at her, defiant. I know I'm being unkind but I can't help myself. I feel like a bottle of Coke that's been wildly shaken up and then unscrewed. All the frustration and resentment I've been feeling for months and months is frothing and bubbling and bursting out of me in an unstoppable stream.

'And another thing: I didn't ask to be an only child,' I continue. 'It's not my fault you're ill and it's not my job to look after you. I just want to be normal, like all my friends, like everyone else. Is that too much too ask? I'm sick of being Little Miss Perfect!' I stop, exhausted, and suddenly self-conscious. I really hope Xavier hasn't heard any of this from upstairs. I must sound like a horrible spoilt brat. Embarrassed, angry and confused, I storm out of the room, slamming the door behind me.

'Well done, Vix,' says Dad, grabbing hold of my arm as I pass. He's been standing in the hall, for I don't know how long, listening. I stop dead in front of him and, unexpectedly, he gives me a little clap. 'Bravo! I'm proud of you.'

Eh? I stare at him, bemused, trying to work out why he appears to be smiling and yet he doesn't sound at all sarcastic. He sounds calm, serious, genuine. His reaction is weird. It's freaking me out. He should at least be angry with me.

'I mean it,' he continues. 'Good for you, Vix. You've been far too much of a goody two-shoes for far too long, putting up with a lot more than someone your age should, never complaining. Now, thank God, you're finally starting to act like a proper teenager, standing up for yourself and showing some spirit. I was beginning to think – to worry – that it might never happen. So, well done. Now, I suggest you go and apologise to your mum, then go up to your room and calm down for a few minutes. I'll smooth things over with her and sort the dinner. OK?'

Chapter 16

Ugly Rumours

My sense of bravado doesn't last for long. Something's going on at school today. Wherever I go, I can sense whispers, hear a low hum of words that I can't quite make out. But I know they're about me. And I know they're not good. Girls chatter away until they notice I'm standing close to them, and then, spontaneously, the conversation seems to dry up. Others will stare at me as I walk by, then turn away and giggle with their friends. I am not imagining this or being paranoid; it's really happening.

At first I wonder if it's about the kiss Xavier gave me outside school; but it can't be because that was last week's news, last week's gossip, and nobody's mentioned it for days. And, anyway, it was just a bit of fun, which nobody (except Rosie and Manon, of course) took seriously. This is something else, something bigger, something nastier. I have no idea what it could be. It's making me feel vulnerable, exposed, the way you do when you dream that you're naked in public. Every time people stare, I find myself looking down my own body to see if I've forgotten to put on my underwear, or have my skirt tucked into my knickers, or if I'm wearing odd socks. It doesn't matter how many times I check and confirm that I'm fully dressed and look fine, I still find myself doing it again.

This is truly horrible. What's that saying Dad always quotes? Something some writer once said, like, 'There's only one thing worse than being talked about and that's not being talked about.' It's not true. I definitely preferred it when I was invisible, a nobody, with a boring life that didn't interest anyone, except my close friends. Now it seems that everyone knows who I am and they all have an opinion about me.

I try to act normally but everyone is being weird with me today, even my friends. They keep giving me sympathetic glances and, even though they're being kind to me, they don't seem to want to chat or to hang out. They're avoiding me. They must know what's being said, and they must feel awkward about it. If I could I'd skive off school for the rest of the afternoon and go home. But I can't. That's one of the (many) problems with having a sick mum. She's always at home. If I turn up unexpectedly, she'll want to know why. And we're not exactly on good terms after our row last night.

At lunchtime, I take myself off to the library. I'm not really hungry and at least it's quiet there, and if anybody does stare I can bury my head in a book and pretend not to see them. I find a heavy hardback about France on the non-fiction shelves and look up Nice in the index. I didn't realise that it's only been part of France for about a hundred and fifty years; before that, it was part of Italy. I make a mental note to ask Xavier about it later, hoping he'll be impressed by my interest. While I read, I sneak chunks of a cereal bar from my bag, which is on my lap under the table, into my mouth, making sure the librarian isn't looking.

I'd stay in the library for the rest of the afternoon, if I could, but I need the loo, and afternoon classes start again in ten minutes. Sighing, I put the book back on the shelf, and head back out into what now feels like enemy territory. I march straight for the toilets, eyes down, head bowed. If I don't make eye contact with anyone, then I can half pretend to myself that this isn't happening.

There's nobody else in the toilets. Relieved, I breathe out. But, as I close the cubicle door behind me, I notice that there's something written on it, some fresh graffiti in bright red marker pen. It draws my eyes towards it, like a magnet. I lean forward, feeling sick as I read. *Vix Fisher . . .* it says, followed by something so disgusting that I'm too embarrassed to repeat it. Fighting back the tears, I try to rub it off with some toilet roll, but it's written in permanent marker and it won't budge. Then I scratch at it with my fingernails, but still it won't shift. The best I can do is to dig around inside my schoolbag for a black biro and scrawl all over it. Although it's still visible, the words are no longer clear.

I rush out of the cubicle and frantically check the others for any more nasty graffiti. When I'm sure that they're clear, I wipe my eyes, take a deep breath and walk out of the toilets, hoping that nobody can tell that I've been crying. That's the worst thing you can do, isn't it, to let people know that they've got to you?

'Can I have a word please, Victoria?' The voice from behind me makes me jump. I twist around. It's Miss Long. She looks stern, purposeful.

'Er, yes. Sure,' I say.

'This won't take a minute.'

She steers me into an empty classroom and closes the door behind her. She doesn't sit down, so I don't either.

'The reason we placed a French boy with you, Victoria, was that we thought that you were one of the most responsible and sensible girls in your year. Unfortunately, that appears not to be the case.'

What does she mean? Is she in on it too? Does she know what people have been saying? Surely she doesn't believe it's true?

'I . . . I don't understand, Miss.'

'Your grades have gone down noticeably since the exchange programme began. You haven't been handing in coursework on time and your teachers say you haven't been concentrating in class. You seem distracted and tired. We're very disappointed in you, Victoria.'

I nod. I'm not sure what she wants me to say. Of course I'm tired, what with going to school and trying to do my homework, looking after my mum, keeping up with my friends and now having a boyfriend all at the same time. It's not easy. It's never been easy. I've always felt a bit like a juggler in a circus, trying to stay upright on a unicycle. I guess the problem now is that I have too many balls to juggle, so it's not surprising if I'm beginning to drop them. But I'm not going to tell Miss Long that. I don't want my teachers to know how much I do for Mum these days, just as I don't want Xavier to know. I don't want anybody to feel sorry for me or for my family or, worse, to interfere.

Miss Long stares at me. 'I'm surprised you don't have anything to say, Victoria.' Maybe she's expecting me to make an excuse, or to argue with her. I'm not used to being told off at school. I don't think it's ever happened before. So I'm not sure how I'm supposed to react.

'I'm sorry,' I mutter. 'I guess I'll try to work harder. And be less tired.'

'Right. Good. Well, I suggest you do knuckle down, Victoria, unless you want us to talk to your parents and consider removing your exchange student.'

God, no! I do not want that. 'I promise,' I say, as she opens the door and releases me back into the corridor. This is truly turning out to be one of the worst days of my life. I have never felt so alone, so got at.

I'm surprised to see Rosie waiting for me outside. She looks concerned.

'I saw Miss Long take you in there,' she says. 'So I waited for you. Are you OK? What did she want?'

'Nothing, really,' I mumble. 'It's not important.'

She peers at me. 'God, you look terrible, Vix. You've been crying. What's up?' She takes my arm. 'Come on, I'm taking you to the sick room. You can't go to class like that. If anyone asks, we'll say you've got really bad period pain, or something.'

I nod, attempting a weak smile, and let her lead me to the sick room. There's no one around, so she helps me on to the bed and sits down next to me. 'So now tell me, what's up?' she says.

I shrug, unsure whether I should tell her, unsure if we're even still close friends. We haven't spoken properly for a couple of days. I can't work out if it's her fault, or mine. Even though nothing's been said, we've stopped walking to school together. It was becoming too awkward, with Manon there. I gulp. 'I didn't think you cared any more.'

'Don't be silly, Vix. Of course I care. Things might be a bit, er, weird, right now, and I'm not a super fan of you being with Xavier, or your PDAs outside school, but you've been my best mate for ever. You know that, right?'

'Yes,' I sob.

'And I don't want you to be upset. Or for French kids to come between us. So, what's going on?' She puts her hand on my shoulder, gently. 'Tell me. Is it Miss Long?'

'Partly that. Partly stuff with my mum. We had a big fight. But no . . . It's more . . . I . . . You must have heard people . . . talking about me.'

She nods. She looks uncomfortable.

'Something's going on. It's horrible. I need to know exactly what they're saying, Rosie.'

'No you don't,' she says. 'It's a load of hurtful crap and you don't want to hear it. Just ignore it and it will all blow over in a few days.'

'I do,' I insist. 'It's driving me mental not knowing. I

just saw some gross graffiti in the loos . . .' I whisper it to her. 'Is it stuff like that?'

Rosie takes a deep breath. 'Yeah, sort of. I'm sorry, hon. OK, well, basically, they're saying that there's only one reason why Xavier likes you. They're saying that you, er, must be giving him something that a French girl wouldn't.'

Horrified, I feel the blood drain from my face. If I didn't look ill enough to be in the sick room before, I must do now. 'Why would they say that about me?' The tears are coming again. I can't do anything to stop them.

Rosie shrugs. 'Because they're nasty girls, with sad little lives, that's why.' She takes a tissue from the box next to the bed and dabs my eyes with it. 'Shush,' she says. 'They're not worth it. Don't cry, Vix.'

'You do know it's not true, don't you, Rosie?'

She widens her eyes. 'Of course I do, silly. I know you. Don't worry, I'm totally on your side on this. I'm going to find out how the rumours started and then I'm going to sort out whoever started them. I bet it's that Lucy Reed. She's been jealous of you from the start because you got a boy. As soon as this period is over, if you're feeling up to it, we'll go and find her. OK?'

I nod, bravely. 'Thank you, Rosie.'

She hugs me. 'No worries.'

Chapter 17

Not the Usual Suspect

We can't find Lucy Reed before the end of school, so Rosie says she'll talk to her tomorrow, and asks me to be patient. I think I can wait one more day to sort this out. Just having Rosie back on side makes me feel so much better: stronger and not so alone. She offers to buy me coffee after school, but Manon will be there and I don't want to talk about this in front of her, so I say I'd rather go straight home. At least I don't look like I've been crying any more, thanks to Rosie's concealer, so I won't have to explain what's up to Mum, or to Xavier.

On the way back I ponder whether I should let

Xavier know what's going on. He is my boyfriend now, and the rumours involve him, so maybe he should know. I decide to listen to my gut and not tell him what people are saying. Not only is it embarrassing but it might make him think badly of me, or question his feelings. Things with Xavier are so lovely and uncomplicated right now that I don't want to dirty them or spoil them by bringing up anything unpleasant. If I did, our little balloon of happiness might pop and being with Xavier would be like the rest of my life: messy and complex, like a knotted ball of string.

Given what people have been saying, I've been thinking a lot about what Rosie suggested the other day: that perhaps I only like Xavier so much because he's French. While I know that's not true, the opposite question has started to bug me: does he only like me because I'm English? Maybe there is something I do that French girls don't – not something gross like *that* – but something I'm not aware of. Or maybe it's just the novelty factor – my accent, or the fact I seem 'exotic' to him (which would be hilarious, as I'm probably the world's least exotic person). I need to know. And, unfortunately, I guess there's only one way to find out. I have to ask him straight out. So, after dinner, when we have a few minutes alone and Xavier moves as if to kiss me, instead of kissing him back I take a deep breath and say: 'Hold on. Why exactly do you like me, Xavier?'

'What eez zis question?' he says. 'I like you because I do. Zat is all. Why do you need to know zis?'

'It's not important,' I lie. 'I just wondered what it is that you like about me.' I know I must sound insecure, like Sky used to when she was dating her horrible ex, Rich, and Rosie and I couldn't understand what she saw in him. Now I know how she must have felt. Except, of course, Xavier hasn't done anything to make me feel insecure. It's all in my own head.

'Zee girls!' he mock scoffs, with a toss of his head. 'Always so many questions. So I must first ask you the same. Why do you like me?'

I giggle, feeling suddenly shy. I'm aware that since I was the one who started this conversation, I have to give him a proper answer. It's actually surprisingly easy to think of reasons. 'OK, then. Because you're cute and kind and fun and I can talk to you, and because you make me laugh, and you make me feel happy.'

'Wow!' he exclaims, and I blush. Was that over the top? Have I gone too far? Maybe he'll think I like him too much. I glance at him and he's beaming, so he must be pleased with what I've said.

'Your turn now, Xavier.'

He chews his lip in thought. 'I like your hairs – and your eyes and your smile. You too make me laugh. I like you also, Veecks, because you are not like zee French girls.'

Oh God . . . he said it. 'What exactly do you mean by that?'

'Many of zem, zey are too, how you say, formal. Not relaxed. And zey moan all zee time. All must be perfect. Nuzzink eez ever right. You are more mature, more gentle, more interesting, more natural. Wiz you I feel comfortable. You are special.'

'Wow!' I say back, realising I'm grinning. 'Thank you. So, when you say French girls moan all the time and stuff, would you say that, er, Manon, and er, her friends, are a bit like that?'

'Manon? *Bof.* She is not important. Why do you always ask about Manon?'

'I don't know . . . She's just an example of a French girl I know, I guess. I don't exactly know many. So is she?'

'Yes, she eez like zat. How you say in *Anglais*, a leetle "up 'erself"?'

I nod, smiling to myself. I feel reassured. 'I see.'

Xavier cups my face. 'Now can I kees you, or do you 'ave more questions?'

'Go ahea—' I begin, but he's already kissing me, and any questions I might have had have vanished from my mind.

I go to bed feeling happier but wake with a start, remembering that today is the day that Rosie and I will confront Lucy Reed about the rumours. I'm dreading going into school again, especially now that I know what people are saying about me, and I'm terrified that I might find some more vile graffiti in the toilets. I half wonder whether I should pretend to be sick, but then I'll be stuck at home all day with Mum, and Xavier won't want to kiss me because he'll think I have germs, and I'll only be delaying the inevitable. *You're strong, Vix,* I tell myself. *You can be brave.*

School isn't as scary as I feared, with Rosie holding my hand all day (not literally, obviously, or that really would start some rumours). Even Manon is quite sweet to me; I figure Rosie must have told her to be nice because I'm having a hard time.

We don't get an opportunity to speak to Lucy Reed until morning break. Rosie spots her in the canteen, queuing up to buy a drink. She's on her own, which is unusual, and it's too good an opportunity to miss.

'Leave the talking to me,' says Rosie, taking charge. 'I don't want you getting upset again.'

'OK . . .'

Rosie strides up to Lucy, purposefully. I tag along,

like a spare part. 'Hey, Lucy,' she says. 'We want to talk to you about something.'

'Ah, it's Rosie Buttery and the notorious Vix Fisher,' Lucy says, smug as ever. 'Well, well, well,' she continues, with a sneer, and I can't help cringing. 'I am surprised to hear what *you've* been up to, Vix. I guess it's true what they say: it's always the quiet ones that you have to watch.'

'Not always,' says Rosie. 'That's what we want to talk to you about.' She waits for Lucy to pay for her drink, then beckons her over to an empty table. 'We know you've been spreading nasty lies about Vix.'

Lucy laughs, which isn't the reaction I was expecting. 'Hey, don't shoot the messenger,' she says, holding up her hands in mock surrender. 'Sure, I heard about Vix, like everyone did, and I might have talked about it with a couple of mates, but I didn't start the rumours and I haven't been going around spreading them. Why would I?'

'Because you're jealous?' says Rosie. 'We know you wanted a boy exchange student and you were pretty pissed off that Vix got one and you didn't.'

'God, that's like so last year's news. It wasn't ever a big deal and I'm so totally over it now. Seriously, guys, I have no problem with Vix and no reason to diss her all over school.' She smiles at me.

Rosie looks puzzled. She glances at me to see my reaction. I think Lucy might be telling the truth, so I nod and shrug my left shoulder.

'OK, so let's say we believe you and you didn't start the lies. Who did?'

'I don't know. All I can tell you is where I heard the story from first.'

'Which is where?' I ask quietly.

'If you really want to know, one of the French girls told me.'

'You're kidding!' exclaims Rosie. 'Who? Your exchange?'

'God, no. She's scared of her own shadow. One of the others. I don't know her name. Cecile, or something like that. No, Camille. You know, the one with the bob and the beaky nose. Seemed really keen to let me know, actually.'

Rosie nods, a grave expression beginning to form on her face. Of course she knows Camille. Camille is one of Manon's closest friends on the trip. She's hung out with her several times. Camille has even been round to Rosie's house. 'Thanks, Lucy,' she says. 'You've been really helpful. Sorry we jumped to conclusions. No hard feelings, eh?'

'Nah,' says Lucy. 'I guess you owe me one.'

'Yeah. Sure.'

We get up from the table and Rosie takes my arm. She's deep in thought and uncharacteristically quiet. But although she doesn't say anything, I know that she's thinking what I'm thinking. If Camille has been spreading the rumours about me, then there's only one place where they could have started.

Manon.

Chapter 18
Plotting Revenge

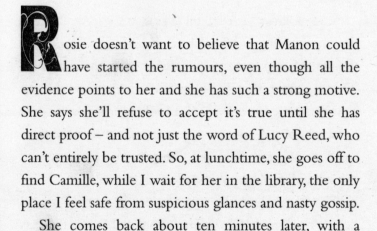

Rosie doesn't want to believe that Manon could have started the rumours, even though all the evidence points to her and she has such a strong motive. She says she'll refuse to accept it's true until she has direct proof – and not just the word of Lucy Reed, who can't entirely be trusted. So, at lunchtime, she goes off to find Camille, while I wait for her in the library, the only place I feel safe from suspicious glances and nasty gossip.

She comes back about ten minutes later, with a serious look on her face. 'It's true,' she whispers. 'Camille said that Manon told all her friends nasty stuff about you and Xavier a few days ago. What a cow.'

I nod. Knowing where the rumours started doesn't help me all that much. I only want to stop them. How do you put the genie back in the bottle once it's out?

'I think we need a meeting to decide how to deal with Manon,' says Rosie. 'You, me and Sky, after school. I'll get rid of Manon somehow. I don't even want to see her, let alone talk to her.'

'OK. I'll text Sky. Maybe we can go to hers.'

'Shhhh,' says the librarian. She walks over to our table. 'If you ladies are going to chat, could you please do it somewhere else?'

'Sorry,' I say, getting up. 'We'll leave now. Come on, Rosie.'

Rosie follows me out, still talking as we leave. It's clear she isn't just upset for me, she's upset for herself too. She thought Manon was a proper friend. Now she feels used. 'Do you know what really gets me? The fact that she was so sympathetic last night, when I told her what was going on at school and how upset you are. She really is so two-faced it's not true. God, she knows we're best mates and she still did it. Maybe she's jealous of us too. God!'

'She does sound like a nasty piece of work.' I hope I don't sound smug. Obviously I won't tell Rosie, but part of me is pleased that I was right all along about Manon. If only I hadn't had to have my suspicions confirmed like this.

Rosie does manage to avoid going home with Manon somehow – I don't ask how – and when school is over we go straight to Sky's flat for 'Crisis Talks' (Rosie always does like to be dramatic). After making small talk with her hippy mum for a few minutes, and declining a cup of wheatgrass tea and a spelt flapjack, we shut ourselves away in her bedroom. It feels so good to have the old gang back together. I know it's only been a few weeks, but it seems like far, far longer. So much has happened since the exchange students arrived. Sky seems super pleased to have us round; I guess she's been feeling very left out lately with Rosie and I wrapped up in our exchanges.

We fill her in on what's been happening. She's open-mouthed.

'God, how awful,' she says, looking at me with sympathetic eyes. 'Poor Vix. Manon sounds like a class-A bitch. I have to say I never liked her. She gave me bad vibes from the first time I met her.'

I stifle a laugh at her complete change of tune, but decide not to pick her up on it, even though she once told me she thought Manon was 'all right'. I do say, 'You sound just like your mum now,' which I know will annoy her.

'No, I don't. Anyway, what the hell are you going to do? Or, rather, what are *we* going to do about her?

Manon's got to pay for what she's done.'

'I tell you what I'd like to do,' says Rosie, who is still very wound up. 'I'd like to throttle her with one of her stupid, perfect scarves.'

'Calm down,' I tell her. 'She is so not worth going to prison over. Even though Holloway Women's Prison is only up the road, so we could visit you a lot.'

'Nah, they'd send her to some juvenile detention centre place in the country, or something,' says Sky. 'She'd hate that.'

'I am here,' says Rosie. 'But good point. Killing her might not be such a great plan.'

Sky concentrates hard. 'OK, then how about we do something a bit more subtle, like persuading her to get a henna tattoo at the market and hoping she has an allergic reaction, like that girl we read about once. Then she'll never, ever be able to dye her hair in the future and one day she'll get really grey, which she'd hate.'

'Yeah!' Rosie says. 'She was really surprised my mum had grey hairs. Apparently nobody in France lets their hair go grey. Ever.'

I shake my head. 'Hmm. Not sure about that. It's a bit complicated. She might not have an allergic reaction, so then she'd just have a cool tattoo and no punishment. And even if she did, we'd have to wait about twenty years for her to get her first grey hairs. Plus, if I'm honest, she doesn't strike me as the tattoo type.'

Rosie nods. 'You're right. We need to be cleverer than that. I know: we could set her up with someone, make her think he really likes her, then get him to laugh at her in front of everyone, so she feels really stupid.'

'Nah,' I say. 'There's only a week till she leaves. We haven't got time. And she's so hung up on Xavier, it probably wouldn't work.'

'True.' Rosie giggles. She's had a silly idea. 'I know. How about asking someone in the art collective to paint an ugly caricature of her on a wall in the street?'

'Nice idea. But why would they do that for us? We can't even get in there.'

'I did,' Rosie reminds us. 'With Rufus Justice, remember? I had a tour and everything.'

'How could we forget?' says Sky, dismissively. That's a story we've heard a few times, and we don't want to hear it again. 'Seriously, though, if we're thinking of getting creative, why not just write some graffiti about her at school?'

I shake my head again. 'She probably wouldn't understand it, if it's in English, and it's too mean. And we might get caught. Bad idea.'

'All right,' says Rosie. 'This is simple. What if you just told Xavier what she's been saying, and got him to say something to her instead? If he told her off and made her feel like she's a horrible person, she'd really hate it. We'd get what we want and wouldn't look bad.'

I really don't like this idea. 'I don't think he'd go for it. It's not really a guy thing. And it's not fair to ask him to fight our battles for us, or to turn against his French friends for us.' The truth is, I still don't feel comfortable with Xavier knowing what's been going on.

The three of us sit silently for a minute or two.

'I can't think of anything else,' says Sky, exasperated. 'Can either of you?'

I sigh. 'No. Rosie?'

'What about the end of exchange party, next Friday night, before they all leave? Your sister is DJing, isn't she, Sky? So she can bring you as her plus one, even though you're not at our school. Maybe we could do something to humiliate Manon there. In public. Make her look stupid or whatever. We've got a week to plot something.'

'Nothing too horrible,' I say. I don't feel comfortable doing anything really mean to Manon. The whole point is to show her we're better than her. 'But, Rosie, you've got to live with her till then. Surely you're not just going to pretend everything is normal?'

'Course not. I'm going to tell her what I think of what she's done and I'll be really frosty too. No more coffees after school or clothes swaps, or late night chats. She can sleep and eat at my house but that's it. In fact, I might just blank her from now on. Not say a word to her. We'll see. And in the meantime we'll come up with a revenge plan for the party.'

I smile. 'OK. Thanks, guys.'

My friends both hug me and I relax, certain that everything is going to work out now.

If only. Before we can even begin to do anything about Manon, something terrible happens.

Chapter 19

The Accident

How did a mundane morning turn into such a nightmare? How, in the time it took me to go to the high street, did my life turn upside down?

Xavier is gabbling at me in French, so fast that I can't make out a single word. Now more than ever I really wish my French was better. 'What is it, Xavier? What's happened? Please tell me.'

I try to make him slow down, to tell me in English, but I don't think he can. He's gripping my wrists, hard, tight. He seems really panicked, white with shock and fear and adrenaline.

'Where 'ave you been?' he manages to say, eventually.

'I called for you, but you did not come.'

I start to apologise, to explain that I was out on the high street, doing some early morning shopping for Mum and I didn't mean to take so long, but stop myself. At this moment, it's really not important. I am much more concerned with what's going on in my street right now, with what might have caused him to be so upset. I am horribly anxious about the fact that there's an ambulance, its lights flashing 'emergency', parked outside *my* house. There's really only one thing it can mean and I absolutely, definitely don't want it to mean that. I am scared. 'Is it my mother, Xavier? Has something happened to her?'

Xavier nods. He seems haunted by whatever it is that he's just witnessed. 'Zair was an accidont, Veecks. She fell.'

'Oh God.' I wrestle my arms from his grip. 'Did you see what happened? Where is she? Is she in the house? In the ambulance?' Before he can reply, I start running towards the ambulance. I sense that Xavier is running behind me but I don't turn around to check. Desperately, I pull at the ambulance doors to find that they're locked. Everyone must be in my house. Perhaps they're working on Mum now. *How long have they been there? Is she . . .? Could she be . . . dead? Shut up, Vix.* I swing around sharply, twisting my ankle on the kerb, and fling myself against my front door, practically falling into the hall. 'Mum!' I shout. 'Where are you? Mum!'

Somehow Xavier is by my side. 'She eez upstairs, in 'er bedroom,' he says, grabbing me again. 'Slow down. The firemen are zair wiz her.'

'Firemen? Is there a fire?' I stop at the bottom of the stairs, confused, only now aware of the sharp pain in my ankle. I can't see or smell smoke and there were no fire engines on the street.

'No, no fire. They try to 'elp her.'

'OK, right, that's good.' I think I understand. I half remember a conversation with Xavier about how in France you call the fire service in an emergency, not an ambulance. The firemen there don't just put out fires, they're paramedics too. Grimacing against the pain, I start to take the stairs two at a time. Xavier rushes behind. 'Hello! Mum! Are you OK? Can anyone hear me?'

A tall, young-looking paramedic greets me on the landing. 'It's OK,' he says. 'Your mum is safe. We're just treating her now and soon we'll take her to hospital.'

Relief courses through my body. She's not dead. I take a deep breath. It feels like the first breath I've taken for minutes, hours. 'I want to see her. Can I come in and see her? Please?'

'It's better if you wait outside for a few minutes with

your friend while we make her comfortable. I promise you she's in good hands.' He nods at Xavier. 'Are you the person who called the ambulance and put her in the recovery position?'

'*Oui*,' says Xavier. He is shaking a little. I put my arm around his shoulder to comfort him. I'd like him to comfort me back, but he doesn't.

'Well done, lad.'

Xavier smiles awkwardly and, for a second, I can see a glimmer of pride shine through his shock. I wonder how he knew what to do. Maybe he learned first aid at school. Thank God he did.

'Yeah, thank you, Xavier.'

'Right, well I'll let you know when we're ready to take her in,' says the paramedic. 'You can come with her in the ambulance. Why don't you both go and wait downstairs?'

Much as I want to see Mum I know he's not going to let me, so I just say, 'OK, thank you.'

He turns away and is about to go back into the bedroom when I'm struck by a thought. 'Hold on a second . . . You do know she has MS, right? It's probably why she fell.'

'No . . . We weren't aware of that.' He beckons me over and asks me to tell him everything I can about her condition. 'Thank you,' he says, when I've finished. 'It would have been helpful if we'd known this before. It explains why she might have fallen. Your French friend didn't tell us.'

'Sorry,' I say, guiltily. 'He doesn't know. He's just staying here for a few weeks.'

Xavier is still waiting for me at the top of the stairs. We go down to the living room together and perch on the end of the sofas, tensely, ready to spring up as soon as the paramedics bring Mum downstairs.

'Veecks, what eez MS?'

He must have overheard me talking to the paramedic. 'It's an illness,' I say matter of factly. I'm not going to lie any more. 'My mum has it. It's why she fell. I'm sorry I didn't tell you before.'

He looks shocked. 'So eet was not an accidont? You tell me she 'urt 'er legs and zat eez why you 'elp 'er at 'ome. She falls before?'

'Yes, she has fallen before. The illness has made her legs not work properly, and now they're very weak too.'

'Why did you not tell me, Veecks?'

'I don't know. I'm sorry. I was . . . embarrassed.'

He can't look at me. 'But why? You left me alone wiz 'er. I was afraid.'

I can't explain my shame about Mum, or put into words how important it is to me to seem normal, like everyone else; I'm aware it doesn't make sense. Now I feel stupid. 'I really, really am sorry.'

I ask him to tell me exactly what happened and, in stumbling English, he does. He says he was still in his bedroom, getting ready, when he heard Mum calling for me. He didn't know I was out, and so didn't do anything at first. Then he heard a tremendous crash from Mum's room. He waited a minute, but nobody else went to her aid. It was then that he realised he was alone in the house, the only one that could help. He pushed open Mum's bedroom door and found her lying next to her bed, unconscious. She had hit her head on something on the way down. Terrified she was dead, he felt for her pulse and put her in the recovery position – something he'd learned through football training. Then he tried to call the emergency services from the phone in her bedroom, but he couldn't remember the number. (They don't call 999 in France.) He went running out into the street, shouting for help. 'Call the firemen! Call the firemen!' A neighbour came out, panicking that the house was burning, and he managed to explain what had happened. She helped him call the ambulance.

I feel dreadful. 'That must have been awful for you, Xavier. I really didn't mean to put you through that. I only went to the shops to get some stuff for Mum. I wasn't out for long. Longer than I should have been but not long.'

He shrugs. 'You should 'ave told me,' he repeats. 'At least I would 'ave been prepared.'

'I know. Again, I'm sorry.' I don't know what else to say. I wish he would look at me, touch me, do something. I can't work out if he's angry or still in shock. What I really need is a hug. I guess he doesn't feel the same.

Our awkward silence is interrupted by the sound of the paramedics coming down the stairs. I rush out into the hall to find them carrying Mum carefully on a stretcher, cautiously taking each step so as not to drop or shake her. I wait for them at the bottom, by the front door.

'Mum? Are you OK?'

She seems drowsy and confused, but when she sees me she tries to smile. I hold her hand for a moment to reassure her.

'Is she going to be OK?'

'She's in good hands, love,' says the second paramedic, who is older and bigger. 'She's come to, now, and she doesn't seem to have done herself any major damage, but the hospital will check her over properly. We just need to get her there as soon as possible.'

'Oh, thank you so much. And it's still OK if I come in the ambulance?'

'Yes, love. You'd better lock up and come now though.'

I turn around. Xavier is standing at the doorway to the hall. 'I have to go in the ambulance with Mum. Will you be OK?'

He shrugs, blankly. '*Oui*, I sink.'

We follow the paramedics out on to the street. Rosie and Manon are standing outside on the pavement, waiting for us. They must have heard what was happening and rushed over. I hesitate at the front door, unsure what to do next. I can't lock Xavier in the house but he doesn't have a key and it's really not safe to leave a house unlocked in Camden Town. And I can't leave him there alone, not when he's in shock. I make a split-second decision. 'Go with Rosie,' I tell him. 'Her mum will look after you till I get back.' He nods.

'We can't wait for you!' calls the paramedic. 'If you're coming, come now.'

'Go!' says Rosie. 'Xavier will be fine.'

'OK, thanks. Oh God!' I'm struck by a sudden realisation. 'Has anyone called my dad? I need to call my dad.'

'Don't worry, my mum will do that. She has his mobile number. Just go. We'll talk later.'

I climb into the back of the ambulance, wincing against the pain of my ankle. It's starting to stiffen up now. Maybe I'll ask someone to look at it at the hospital, later. Mum is lying with her eyes closed, an oxygen mask over her mouth and nose. She seems so fragile and vulnerable; she even appears to have shrunk. I feel that anxious, nauseous sensation again, even though I know she's not in immediate danger.

As the ambulance doors shut, I look out on to my street. The last thing I see is Manon's smiling face, her arms wrapped tightly around Xavier's back, as she comforts him. Her expression doesn't look to me like one of compassion, or sympathy, or even concern. It's one of jubilation: she thinks she's finally won. And then the siren comes on and we speed away to the hospital.

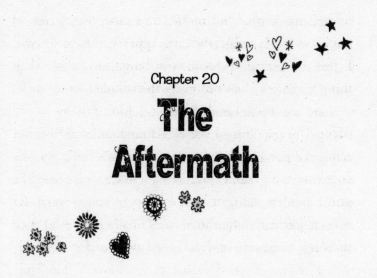

Chapter 20
The Aftermath

ad drives me home from the hospital late in the evening. Exhausted, we don't talk much. We've been told that, although Mum doesn't have any serious injuries from her fall, she's likely to be kept in for several weeks. Tomorrow or the next day, once she's over the concussion, they'll transfer her to the neurological unit and treat her for her relapse, and then rehabilitate her with physiotherapy. Dad looks drained and anxious and I want to reassure him, but I don't know how. I reach over and stroke his arm, uselessly, until he has to change gear, and I snatch my hand away.

We're almost home, stuck in traffic on Parkway, when

he hits me with a bombshell. 'I'm sorry, Vix, but as you've probably guessed, Xavier can't stay here for the rest of the exchange. Most of the time now, I'm either going to be with your mum at the hospital or at work, so there will be nobody to look after him.'

No, I haven't guessed. Maybe I'm stupid, but until he says this, I haven't even thought of this possibility. I'm so used to coping alone – cooking, cleaning, shopping – that I figured things could carry on pretty much as normal, just with Mum in hospital, instead of on the sofa or in her bedroom. How am I going to make things up with Xavier, and spend his last week with him, if he's not staying at my house?

Before I can open my mouth to say that I can manage fine all by myself, Dad pre-empts me. 'And don't even think about suggesting that you stay in the house together, with no adult supervision. That's not going to happen. However mature and trustworthy you are – usually – the school wouldn't allow it. And nor will I. You are only fourteen. I'm afraid I have already spoken to Miss Long and it's been agreed that Xavier is going to join one of the other French boys at his English family's home. They're coming to pick up his stuff tomorrow. I've also spoken to Sky's mum and she's very happy for you to stay there on the nights that I'm not around.'

'Buh . . .' I begin, desperately and pointlessly, when I

know it's already a done deal. I want to say how ridiculous it is that I'm suddenly being treated like a child, when for so long I've been the one looking after Mum. If anything had happened during the nights while Dad was away, I'd have had to be the responsible one, the one in charge, the grown-up. Mum hasn't looked after me for years. 'Buh . . .'

'No buts,' says Dad. 'It's all decided. So you're just going to have to live with it. I'm sorry.'

I'm too tired to argue and I know it would be hopeless. It's just not fair. I turn away from him, sulking. Why act like an adult if you're not being treated like one?

Eventually, I ask, 'Will I at least get to say goodbye to Xavier?'

'I'm sure you can have a few minutes with him when he comes to get his things.'

'A few minutes?'

'Yes, Vix. Leave it for now, will you? There are other, more important things we need to talk about.'

At this moment, nothing feels more important than sorting things out with Xavier. I'm terrified that he hates me and, what would be worse, certain that I've delivered him straight into Manon's clutches. If only he had a damn phone with him, so I could at least text him. I don't even know where he's staying. I sigh. 'Like what?'

'Like the future.' He sounds grave. 'Things really are going to have to change, love. We can't all carry on like this any more. Whether your mum likes it or not, when she comes out of hospital we're going to have to get some proper outside help in. Properly qualified nursing care. For your benefit, as much as hers. We've discussed it before, but she's been very resistant. And if there's any way we are going to avoid moving, we need to make some modifications to the house too – hoists and stairlifts and things. We can't risk another accident like this one.'

I nod. I can't cope with the thought of change right now. I certainly can't deal with the idea – however remote – of leaving Paradise Avenue and my friends, maybe even leaving Camden. Saying that aloud, though, would sound selfish. Instead I say, 'Mum is really going to hate that.'

'I know she is, love. She's as stubborn as you are. Funny that, eh? But needs must.'

We sit, silently, lost in our own thoughts, for the rest of the journey.

The house seems eerily empty and quiet without Mum or Xavier. It makes me want to switch on all the lights and put the radio or TV on in every room for company. Dad gets some Indian food delivered for dinner, but it's a waste because we can only pick at it. I go to bed early, exhausted, my ankle still throbbing (it's sprained), first texting Rosie and Sky to let them know Mum is OK. I can't stay awake long enough to see if they reply.

In the morning I have messages from both of them – sweet, reassuring messages. Sky says her room is my room, whenever I want it. Rosie asks if she can come round to see me today. I don't even ask Dad if it's OK; I just tell her yes, come as soon you can.

She arrives soon after lunch and I take her straight up to my bedroom. We talk through Mum's accident and I tell her how awful I feel that I left Xavier alone with her, even though I had no idea she would fall. I admit I probably haven't been completely honest about how sick Mum is. Rosie tells me I'm silly; she and Sky would have helped more, if only they'd known. She says they're going to look out for me more from now on and, if I'm ever not coping, I should say. I try to change the subject; this sort of attention embarrasses me. And, anyway, I need to know about Manon and Xavier.

'So what happened after I went off in the ambulance? With Xavier and Manon?'

'Nothing. Xavier came back to ours, and my mum called Miss Long and she came to pick him up about an hour later. I think he went to stay with one of his friends last night.'

'Oh, so he didn't stay with you?' That's good. At least he wasn't with Manon all evening. 'Was he OK?'

'He was pretty shaken up at first, really quiet, but he was fine after a while. Actually, he was really worried about your mum, and you. My mum spoke to your dad at the hospital and told him everything was OK.'

'That's nice of him. And what about Manon? Were they . . . together when they were round at your house?'

'Together? No! Don't be silly.'

'It's just, when I left, they were all over each other and it looked like . . . And he was so angry with me.'

'God, Vix, give Xavier some credit. He's with you. He really likes you. He's not going to get with Manon in the space of five minutes, especially when your mum's just been rushed to hospital in an ambulance. I can't believe you even thought that.'

Looking at it like that, I suppose she's right. No decent guy would do that, and Xavier is a decent guy. I feel stupid and disloyal for jumping to conclusions. 'Yeah, I guess. But it wouldn't stop Manon, would it? We already know she's a nasty, amoral cow.'

Rosie raises her eyebrows. She knows it's not like me to be so mean or bitchy about anyone. To tell the truth, I'm quite shocked myself at how much hatred and anger I feel towards Manon. 'Hmm,' she says, clearly deciding that in the circumstances she won't comment on it.

'Listen to me, Vix. Xavier doesn't want to be with Manon. I saw what happened. He just needed to talk to someone in French, to get stuff off his chest, and she just happened to be there. That's all.'

'Do you really think so?'

'Yeah. Imagine if it was the other way round. If you were really shocked and upset about something really traumatic that had just happened, would you want to have to translate all your feelings into French before you got it off your chest? I know I wouldn't. You'd just want to let it out to the first English person you saw.'

'True, I guess. So what did Manon say about it all? About Xavier? I'm sure she wasn't that sensitive.'

'Well . . . she seemed pretty smug right afterwards — like she thought he was in to her — but, to be honest, I don't think he's spoken to her since he left last night. She hasn't mentioned anything to me — and she would have done. And, think about it: if he won't be staying on the street any more, she's not even going to see much of him now, is she? So don't worry.'

'I know I shouldn't. But I can't help it.' I look down at the floor, ashamed. I hate myself for worrying about Xavier, about whether he still wants to be with me, when the only person I should be worrying about is Mum. God, I must be the most self-centred, horrible person in the world.

'Of course you can't. Especially after what she did to you at school. Do you still want me to confront her about the gossip? Do you still want to get her back? With everything that's happened, it sort of got forgotten. But I'm up for it, if you are.'

'No point,' I say, without even having to think about it. Suddenly, much as I dislike her, what Manon did to me seems like ancient news. 'I don't care. Say something if you want. Don't if you don't. Getting revenge on her doesn't seem all that important any more.'

Rosie chews her lip. 'We'll see. I've got to live with her for almost another week, remember. I might do something, I might not. She already knows I'm pissed off with her and, whatever happens, I'm not going to hang out with her from now on. No more coffees or market trips.'

'OK.'

Rosie hugs me. 'I'm really sorry I didn't see what she was like when she first came here. I should have listened to you. I guess I got carried away with the whole French style thing.'

'S'OK.'

'Just don't stress about Manon. She's the least of your worries.'

I wish she wasn't right.

Dad takes me to see Mum for a couple of hours in

the afternoon. She tries to put on a brave face for us but I can tell she's really down about what's happened, and about being stuck in hospital. I don't know how to make her feel better. It's not really a grapes and 'get well soon' situation. She's not going to get well – not properly anyway – and she hates grapes, unless they're crushed and alcoholic and come in a bottle, and wine doesn't mix too well with her medication. Still she seems happy to see me.

At last, in the early evening, Xavier comes around to pack up his belongings and take them to his new exchange family's house. I'm too nervous to let him in, so I stay upstairs in my room while Dad does it. I hear voices – too many voices – and then the stomping of too many feet up the stairs. He must have brought his French friend along, and maybe the English host boy as well. I'm not going to get any time alone with him, am I? Why couldn't the others have waited downstairs? Can't Xavier pack his rucksack on his own? He doesn't have that much stuff! Or is he avoiding me deliberately? I loiter in my bedroom, wondering whether I should come out and make my presence known, or pretend I'm not even home. Procrastinating, I lie on my bed, listening while drawers are opened and shut, hearing laughter and chatter, but finding it impossible to make out what anyone is saying. Then I hear the spare-room door click shut and there are heavy footsteps on the stairs again.

He's gone; I'm too late. That's it, then. Gutted, I curl up on my bed and curse myself for mucking everything up, and for being a coward and missing my last proper chance to speak to him. I feel like crying, but I can't.

Unexpectedly, there's a knock on my door. It makes me jump and I swing up from my bed so fast that I feel light-headed. 'Er, come in,' I say, in a high-pitched, wimpy voice, that doesn't sound like me.

Xavier peers around the door. The sight of him makes my heart beat furiously. 'Veecks, I 'ave come to say *au revoir*,' he says. He seems off with me, not cold exactly, but cool, and I can't tell if it's because he's still angry or because people are waiting for him.

'You can come in properly, if you like,' I say, pulling the door open wide for him. I smile, hoping that if I'm friendly he'll warm up too. 'We can have a chat.'

It doesn't work. He stays put by the door, looking behind him. 'Zair is not time. I am sorry. I must go now.'

'Oh. That's a shame. I wanted to talk to you about yesterday. I wanted to say sorry.'

He appears uncomfortable. 'It eez OK. But I must go.'

'OK, I understand.' I'm not sure if I should walk towards him, or stay inside my room. I take a step forward, but he doesn't move.

'Bye, Veecks,' he says, raising his hand in a wave. 'I'll

see you soon.' He doesn't touch me or even give me two kisses on my cheeks. Complete strangers do that in France!

I don't manage to finish saying the word 'goodbye' before he turns around and heads back down the stairs. I feel horrible: flat, empty and miserable. It's hard to believe that just a couple of days ago our lips were virtually glued together and that I felt closer to him than I've ever felt to anyone. I suppose I should be grateful that he hasn't broken up with me.

At least, I don't think he has. Has he?

Chapter 21
The End of Exchange Soirée
(That's French for 'party')

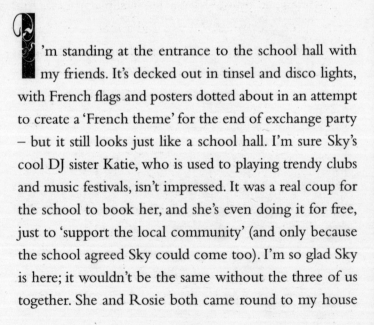

I'm standing at the entrance to the school hall with my friends. It's decked out in tinsel and disco lights, with French flags and posters dotted about in an attempt to create a 'French theme' for the end of exchange party – but it still looks just like a school hall. I'm sure Sky's cool DJ sister Katie, who is used to playing trendy clubs and music festivals, isn't impressed. It was a real coup for the school to book her, and she's even doing it for free, just to 'support the local community' (and only because the school agreed Sky could come too). I'm so glad Sky is here; it wouldn't be the same without the three of us together. She and Rosie both came round to my house earlier, to try to help take my mind off Mum and Xavier and to get me in a party mood. We had a mini pre-party while we got dressed and did our make-up, playing music and dancing around my bedroom. It really did help.

I'll admit that, several times this week, I decided I wasn't even going to go to the party, but Rosie refused to let me back out. She said Mum would hate me to miss out on something fun just because she was in hospital, and it was pretty clear that the gossip about me at school has died down entirely since people heard about her accident, so I shouldn't worry about that, either. She also said she might possibly have let it slip – quietly and strategically (i.e. to Lucy Reed and a few others) – that Manon wasn't to be trusted, which helped my cause. As for Xavier, both Rosie and Sky said that I'd regret forfeiting my last chance to see him and, hopefully, smooth things over before he goes home. They're right, I guess. So here I am.

Rosie, Sky and I walk into the hall together, arm in arm. I'm trying to feel as confident as I must look, even though underneath I'm terrified. The room is already half full with girls from my year at school and boys from our local 'brother' school, plus their exchange students. There's no sign of Xavier yet, or Manon. I wonder if they'll arrive together. That would be horrible. But, at least, nobody gives me a funny look or turns away to whisper, so Rosie must be right: the wave of gossiping really has passed for good. I relax a little. Rosie and Sky have told me I look good. I'm wearing my favourite black skinny jeans and a vintage lace top that I found in the market. Sky has on some luminous leggings and a tight jersey tunic, and Rosie is parading about in a geometric print shift dress from the nineteen-sixties, which she bought in one of the charity shops on the high street. 'It was only five pounds,' she keeps saying, when anyone compliments her on it. It's getting a bit boring now.

We help ourselves to some drinks and crisps from the food tables, and catch up with a few of our friends. Nobody is dancing yet; it's far too early and far too embarrassing to be the first. The French kids seem to be hanging out with their French friends, and the English ones, likewise. As parties go, it feels a bit flat, a bit forced. I look around the hall and wonder how many of these people will even remember their exchange students' names in a few months, let alone keep in touch.

Sky nudges me. 'Look!' she whispers. 'On the left. Oh. My. God.'

I turn around as subtly as I can, to see what she means. Walking into the room as if she's on a catwalk is Manon. She's wearing a full-length, one-shouldered evening gown, with skyscraper heels and her hair in a chignon.

Two of her friends follow behind, like bridesmaids.

'Wow! What does she have on? She looks like she's getting married or something. Or going to the Oscars.'

'I think she looks like a toddler who has raided her mum's dressing-up box,' says Sky. 'Where did she even get that dress?'

'I know,' says Rosie, smirking. 'I did try to tell her it wasn't *that* kind of party. OK, maybe not as hard as I could have, because frankly she deserves to look a bit stupid, but I did mention that we would all be quite casual. She thought she knew better, as usual.'

Sky looks doubtful. 'Own up, Rosie. I know you! Did you really try to talk her out of it or did you set her up?'

Rosie gives her a bashful smile. 'OK, if I'm honest, I might just have told her how fabulous she looked when she tried on her outfit last night. But I didn't make her choose it or wear it. Does that make me a terrible person?'

'No! I think it's great,' says Sky. 'It means we sort of got our revenge on her after all, without even trying, or having to do anything really mean. She did it to herself.'

We turn to look at Manon again. She's scanning the room, an expression of growing bewilderment on her face. It seems to be dawning on her, that far from being the belle of the ball, she sticks out like a great big, bright red, French thumb. Her haughty stance has vanished and now she's looking decidedly uncomfortable, her shoulders hunched, her arms wrapping themselves around her middle in a gesture of protection. I almost feel sorry for her. Almost.

Sky nudges me again. 'Don't turn around but Xavier is coming in.' She grips my hand. 'It'll be fine. Just be brave.'

I ignore her and, unable to stop myself, spin around to look. My heart is beating so fast that I feel dizzy. Xavier is with a couple of French boys. It's the first time I've seen him properly for days, and he looks lovely, all smart and clean, his hair gelled back and his shoes polished. I've missed him so much. I wonder if he's missed me too.

My heart sinks; he's heading in Manon's direction. I guess it really is over, then. She's won. Rosie was wrong. They've probably been meeting up in secret over the past week. I don't think I can stay at this party all evening, watching the two of them together. It might kill me. I think I should . . .

But wait . . . maybe I'm mistaken. Xavier isn't stopping at Manon's side; he's just nodded at her and said something inaudible, and now he's walking straight past her. I think he might be coming over towards me. Oh my gosh. He's coming to talk to me. I turn to my friends for support, but Rosie and Sky have drifted away from my sides.

'Veecks,' he says, there before I'm prepared. He's smiling, warm like he used to be.

'Xavier,' I reply, like an idiot.

''ow are you?' Three kisses. 'I am pleased to see you. 'ow eez your muzzer?'

'She's much better,' I tell him. 'Still in hospital and probably will be for a while, but doing much better.'

'I am glad,' he says.

'Listen. I know I've said it before but I really am genuinely sorry about what happened. About not telling you how bad my mum was. About you having to find her and call the ambulance all on your own. About you not being able to stay with my family any more. About everything.'

'Eet eez OK. I am not angry now.'

'Honestly?'

'*Oui.*'

'So you forgive me?'

'But of course. I only wish you 'ad told me before.'

'I know. I'm sorry. I sort of screwed things up.'

He shrugs and smiles. 'Even you, Veecks, you are only 'uman.'

I giggle. 'I guess so.'

'You look very beautiful tonight.'

That makes me blush and beam at the same time. 'Really? Er, thank you. So do you. Handsome, I mean.'

'*Merci.*' He grins.

'Um . . .' I'm not feeling brave at all, but I need to say this: 'I miss you.'

'Me also,' he says, in a sad, gentle voice. 'I steel care about you, Veecks.'

Neither of us knows what to say then. We stand staring at each other, until we both feel too awkward to maintain eye contact and look down at the floor instead. I watch the coloured disco lights bouncing in rhythmic patterns on the lino and will him to say something, or do something, because my mind has gone totally blank.

'We should dance,' he says eventually, taking both of my hands in his.

'But there's no one else on the dance floor yet. Everyone will stare at us.'

'So? I care not. You do?'

I do, but I don't tell him that. At least I know I'm an OK dancer so I won't make too much of a fool of myself. I let him lead me on to the middle of the dance floor and try to relax and let my body go with the beat. My ankle is still a little sore, but it doesn't hurt to put weight on it any more. If I close my eyes, I can forget about everyone else. Soon I start to enjoy myself. I open my eyes and Xavier grabs me and spins me around, laughing. It's quite hard to keep up with him. He's a little . . . clumsy. To tell the truth, I think he's got two left feet, which only makes me like him more. It wouldn't do for Mr Perfect to be too perfect, would it? I notice, with relief, that other people are beginning to join us on the dance floor. Rosie and Sky sidle up to me and take it in turns to dance with me. This is the most fun I've had in ages.

I don't know how long we dance for but it must be a long time because I'm thirsty and my feet hurt and I really wish I'd ignored Rosie's advice and put on my Converse tonight. I'm about to suggest to Xavier that we get a drink and sit down when I hear a familiar riff. It can't be . . . It is! It's 'You're The One That I Want' from *Grease*! This is not the sort of record Katie usually plays – it's much too old and far too uncool. Rosie and Sky must have requested it for me. Remind me to kill them both later.

Xavier and I look at each other and giggle. Naturally, we start singing along in our best yogurt. 'Ya da wada wada. You da wada wada. Ooh ooh ooh, allai,' before collapsing into laughter.

'Sank you,' he says, giving me a big bear hug.

I have a sudden urge to mark this moment for ever. 'Take a photo of us on your phone, Rosie, please,' I beg.

'Sure,' she says, directing us into a pose. 'Say cheese. Or should that be *fromage*?'

Once the flash has gone off, Xavier pulls me towards him and into a deep, passionate kiss – right there and then, in the middle of the dance floor. I wasn't sure he'd ever kiss me again, and it feels incredible. When we break off he holds me close, his heart beating as fast as mine. Over his shoulder, out of the corner of my eye, I can see Manon. She is dancing with her friends, a sulky expression on her face. Her dress is so tight that she can barely move her legs. She's clearly not having a good time at all. Shame. I close my eyes and blot Manon out, allowing myself to melt into another kiss. And then another. And another. I forget about wanting a drink, or having sore feet, or even that I'm at a party with practically everybody I know.

But then Katie's voice interrupts the music to tell us that it's time for the very last track of the night and that our parents and hosts will be waiting for us in the corridor by the main school doors. It hits me that Xavier won't be coming home with me tonight and that tomorrow he will be getting the train back to the airport, and flying back to Nice.

We kiss again. It is just as wonderful as all the others, just as sweet and soft. But there is something different about this kiss, something which only strikes me later, long after it has ended, when I'm home and tucked up in bed. This kiss feels like the end of something.

Rosie taps me on the shoulder. 'Sorry to, er, interrupt but your Dad's here, Vix. And I reckon they're going to put the hall lights back on in about thirty seconds.'

'Thanks,' I say, noticing for the first time that the music has stopped and there's hardly anybody left in the room. 'Tell him I'm coming. You'd better find your friend, Xavier.'

He nods. '*Merci* for a wonderfool night, Veecks.'

I smile. 'Thank you too.' I take a deep breath. It's now or never. 'Will you keep in contact when you're back in France? We could email or instant message. I could give you my address.'

'Maybe,' he says. 'I will try. Per'aps. But I am not so good at writing in *Anglais*. I prefer to talk. And the phone, eet eez difficult for me, and expensive.'

He doesn't ask for my address or offer me his. He's letting me down gently, I think. Maybe that's better than believing and hoping that we'll stay in touch, and then being disappointed when it fizzles out – feeling gutted when one day I send a message and he simply doesn't reply. It still hurts, though.

I smile again, so he can't tell how gutted I am. 'I do understand. Listen, maybe you'd rather I didn't – and I know you're not staying at mine any more, but would it be all right if I came to say goodbye at the station tomorrow?'

'Of course,' he says. 'Yes, I would like zat.'

And, with that, the fluorescent lights flicker back on, and the magic evaporates.

Chapter 22

Adieu

I come to St Pancras alone, by bus. Rosie hasn't come to see Manon off; she made an excuse not to, so she didn't have to pretend she was sad to say goodbye. 'Good riddance to bad rubbish,' she said, earlier, when I asked her about it. She was as dramatic as ever. 'I'm going to ritually burn the scarves I bought as soon as she's out of here. I can't wait to see the back of her. And I hope I never, ever see her again, as long as I live.' She's not the only one; three cheers to that! I think Rosie's dad – who is wise enough not to ask too many questions about the frosty atmosphere between his daughter and her exchange – is bringing Manon by car. Honestly, I don't care how she gets here, as long as she isn't on my street when I arrive home.

We meet at the entrance to the station nearest the airport train. Xavier is standing alone, away from his group, waiting for me, and that makes me feel happy. He really does want to say goodbye. He really does care, even if it did just turn out to be a holiday romance, after all. Even if I'll probably never hear from him again.

He grins as I approach him and my stomach lurches. I'm going to miss that sensation, I realise, even though it's weird and uncomfortable.

'So, Veecks,' he says, planting three tingly kisses on my cheeks. 'So, zis eez goodbye.' He says it in his French, matter-of-fact, 'that's life' tone. I know it doesn't mean he isn't sad, but I can't help wishing he appeared more upset.

'I guess it is,' I say, hoping he hasn't noticed my watery eyes. 'It's gone so fast.'

'*Oui*, eet's true. Too fast. I very much liked Camden, and London too.'

'Good. I'm glad.' I'm finding it really hard to know what to say or look directly at him. I'm worried that if I express how I feel, I might start bawling.

'Maybe you'll come to Nice sometime, to veesit.'

'Sure, I'd like that. And maybe you'll come back to London. To Camden Town. There's so many places I never got to show you in the end. Mum should be better by then and you can stay and . . .' I tail off. 'Anyway.'

'I hope so. One day, per'aps.'

He glances at his watch and I realise I'm running out of time. If I don't say something now, I never will. 'I've really loved having you here, Xavier,' I blurt out. 'It's been . . . I know it all went a bit weird at the end, but I couldn't have asked for . . . a better French exchange student.' Yes, I've chickened out. But how can I tell him how special he is to me when he clearly doesn't feel the same? He'll think I'm an idiot. A pathetic idiot.

He nods. '*Merci*. I am happy that I met you too, Veecks. Please say goodbye and sank you again to your parents.'

So that's all I'm getting – he's happy that he met me. I was right not to say anything more. 'Of course I will. They're really sorry they couldn't come to the station to see you off.'

'Sank you.'

We're distracted by movement and noise behind us. The French exchange coordinator is gathering all the French students together, taking a register to make sure everyone is accounted for. She motions to Xavier to come over. She looks impatient.

'I sink that I must go now,' he says.

'Yeah, I know.'

He sighs and clutches my hand. 'Goodbye, Veecks.'

'Goodbye, Xavier.'

There's no time for a proper kiss now and, anyway, everybody is watching us, pointing to their watches, waiting for him. So it's going to end with a quick peck on both my cheeks. The way it all began. The kiss at the party really was the very last one. If only I could have one more, just one more . . .

'*Au revoir.*' He lets go of my hand and gives me a smile. I smile back, as bravely as I can, even though I want to cry. And then he picks up his rucksack, swings it on to his shoulder and walks away to join his his French friends. I stare at his back, watching his rucksack bob along until he's disappeared into the group, and then turn away, unsure what to do with myself. I feel lost, hopeless and very alone. Maybe I'll grab a coffee or look around the station shops – anything to distract myself, to avoid going home. I start to walk away, slowly, aimlessly.

'Veecks! Wait!'

There's a hand on my shoulder. It can't be? Can it?

'Xavier? I . . . I . . .' Somehow, impossibly, he is by my side again. 'I thought I would never . . . that you'd gone!' I'm so surprised and confused that I realise my feet are still walking.

He runs in front of me, grinning. 'Stop! We 'ave only two minutes. Come!' He grabs my arm and manoeuvres me to the side of the information desk, where we're out of sight. 'I 'ave somesing for you.' He presses a piece of paper into my palm and closes my hand over it. 'Eet ees my email address. If you steel want. And my telephone numbair.'

'Seriously? You want me to contact you? I thought at the party you said . . .'

'*Oui*. Eef you steel want. Eet won't be easy, but, eef possible I want to try. I realise I care about you very much, Veecks. And I will mees you. A lot.'

I'm so happy I can barely breath. 'Wow! Me too. I wanted to tell you before but I didn't think you felt the same. I . . .'

'Shush,' he says, putting his index finger on my lips. 'Or zair will be no time for zees . . .

Before I can say 'For what?' his mouth is on mine and he is kissing me so hard, so deeply that I feel dizzy.

Just as I start to understand what's happening, to enjoy it and kiss him back, he pulls away. *Just one more kiss,* I think again. *Just one more . . .*

'And now I must really go!' he says. 'Goodbye! *Au revoir! A bientôt!* Email me!' And then he's off, running towards the platform, as fast as he can, weaving his way through the crowds. For one brief moment, as he walks through the ticket barrier, he turns around and gives me a little wave. I wave back, but he doesn't see me.

My boy from France has gone.

I stand rooted to the spot for a few minutes, unable to decipher my emotions. Did that really just happen, or did I imagine it? It must have done, I can still feel the imprint of his lips. He does care about me and want to keep in touch – that's amazing. But he's not here any more. I am both happier and more sad than I've ever felt before. It's hard to believe that it's only been a month since I stood here with Dad, waiting for my unknown French exchange, expecting nothing at all. So much has happened. So much has changed. I've changed.

I take a deep breath. I don't want to go back to my house and I don't feel like going to the hospital to see Mum right now, but I can't stand here for ever, holding back the tears, trying to look normal.

'Vix!' Rosie rushes up to me, from nowhere, out of breath. She has Sky with her. The two of them hug me. 'Thank God you're still here. Are you OK? We thought you'd need cheering up. So we came down to the station to find you. It took us a while and we were worried you might have gone already.'

'That's really nice of you both,' I say. I've never felt so relieved to see anybody in my life. 'I feel a bit . . . upset.' My voice cracks.

'Of course you do, hon,' says Sky. 'But it's going to be fine, I promise. Come on, let's get a coffee and you can tell us all about it. Then we'll get the bus back to

Camden and go shopping or something.'

'Thanks, I'd like that.'

Rosie links her arm through my right arm, and Sky takes the left. I feel stronger and safer already. As we move off, I take one last look behind me, at the empty platform, at the spot where Xavier stood just a few minutes ago, and I wonder when I'll see him again. Then I turn my head forwards, towards Camden, to the future, and I think – I know – that, somehow, everything is going to be all right.

Acknowledgements

Thank you to my agent Catherine Pellegrino and to the team at Piccadilly press: Brenda Gardner, Anne Clark, Melissa Hyder, Andrea Reece, Margot Edwards, Vivien Tesseras, Geoff Barlow, Lea Garton, Simon Davis and Geoffrey Lill.

It's been a year of drama, trauma and huge changes in my life, and a year that I wouldn't have survived without the incredible support and love of my family and friends, notably my parents, Michael and Vivien Freeman, Judy Corre, Claire Fry, Nicola Rossi, Jax Donnellan, Diane Messidoro, Karen John-Pierre, Rachel Baird, Nishi Shah, Miriam Herman, Gabbie Lecoat, Anna Smith, Colin Richardson, Vicki Prais and Jo Cotterill.

I'm sorry I can't name everyone here – I really would need another book to do so. Thanks to Ella Garai-Ebner and Orli Vogt-Vincent for their enthusiasm and input.

And finally, a *grand merci beaucoup* and *gros bisous* to Mickaël Lorinquer.